Moon Inherits the Sky

T. RENEE

Dedication

This book is dedicated to one of the loves of my life, Taylor Alexis Dumpson-Lippencott. Taylor, my tiny little titan, my love for you is as infinite as the night sky. You are truly an amazing woman, friend and family member. Your ambition, integrity, strength and love know no bounds. When I think of what it means to be courageous, I think of you. I love you always and forever.

Prologue

"You're making a mistake. Why don't you listen to your mother? I know you, Moon. Nobody knows you like I do."

"Mama, honestly, sometimes I feel like you don't know me at all."

The silence that followed Ehnita's last statement was not because she felt regret or wanted to reel back the words that had fallen from her mouth. The silence was because Ehnita wanted to give her mother the opportunity to change the course of the conversation. As hurtful as her statement may have been, Ehnita was too annoyed to notice her mother's pain. But if she had noticed, she would have reasoned it was her mother's own fault for making her feel that way.

"Why do you do this, Mama? You know it bugs me when you call me that. Every single time we speak, I have to tell you the same thing again and again. If you can't call me Ana, can you at least call me by my real name? I'll take Ehnita over Moon any day of the week."

"I do call you by your *real* name. Your name, Ehnita, in our language means Moon. I call you by the name that I have given you. It is you who uses a fake name. This *Anita, Ana* person that you tell people you are. *That* is not your name. *That* is not who you are."

"That is me, Mama. Like I said, you don't know me."

Every single day, Ehnita and her mother, Oneida, would talk to each other on the phone, and no matter how the conversation started, it would always end the same…in an argument. The argument was always around identity, both Ehnita's and Oneida's, and both sides would layer the conversation thick with disapproval, sorrow, and guilt about who they thought the other person was and should be.

Their arguments were as constant as the winds were over troubled water, as routine as the sun and the moon trading places each day. Their daily disagreement had become their ritual, but theirs was ineffectual; it produced nothing, it resolved nothing, and it was without end.

As expected as their current conversation was, and as routine as it may have felt, today Ehnita was in no mood to entertain it. As she closed her eyes and took in a breath, Ehnita smiled to herself and let her last statement linger in the air. Her statement had been sharp, but it had also been the truth…her mother didn't know her. Her mother knew Moon. She knew the person she wanted Ehnita to be, but she never knew Ana—the person she was in that moment—and right then, on the eleventh floor of her high-rise luxury building, Ana felt like she had finally won the war.

It wasn't Moon with the expensive condo, lucrative job, and fancy clothes; it was her. It was Ana. Her whole life she felt as if she were in constant competition with herself, but today the race was over. Today she had tasted victory, and she had done it her way, as Ana, in spite of all her mother's pleading and rooting for Moon.

Tonight, Ehnita was celebrating. She wasn't a fool, though. She knew that mourning Moon was something her mother would do, but she assumed with this kind of news that the mourning would be put off for at least a day, and her mother would give her at least five minutes of excitement and celebration. But, once again, Ehnita was wrong.

Oneida did not want to celebrate. She was not overjoyed; despair echoed in the moments of silence between them like a drum, like a slowly breaking heart—each thud filled with more pain and sorrow than the one that came before it. The news this evening of Ehnita's pending nuptials brought a terrible sadness to Oneida's heart.

"You do not know yourself, Moon. I know you better than anyone. This Ben, he is not the man for you."

"How would you even know that, Mama? You've never met him."

"I know this because I know this man does not call you by your name. I know this because I have not met him. I know this because he has not come to meet me. I know this because *I know* he does not know you, not the real you, and how can he when you do not even know yourself?"

"He works, Mama. He's busy. No one has time to drive out to the reservation to sit with you on those narrow pieces of wood you call steps and chat all day." Ehnita sighed as she threw her free hand up in the air and shook her head. "Why can't you be happy for me?"

"Because you will not be happy with him."

"I am happy, Mama."

"Oh, my precious Moon. You do not know what happiness is. You do not know what it feels like to find the one you are meant to be with and feel pure joy."

Ehnita chuckled as she let her head fall back and rest on the arm of the sofa. "What do you know about it anyway, Mama? You've been single as long as I've been alive."

"If you are lonely, Moon, come home, come home to me. Don't marry a man that is not right for you."

"You want me to come home and stay with you so that we can be alone together? I don't think so. Why don't *you* move off the reservation and come live in the city? I can get you your own place, something much better than what you have now."

"Who says it will be better? You want me to leave my people, my land, my family… How will this make things better?"

"You'll be closer to your daughter. The people on the res will understand, and it's not like you wouldn't be able to go back and visit."

"This is my home, Ehnita. I will not leave."

"So, you're choosing the reservation over your own daughter? Nice, Mama, real nice."

"Never, Ehnita. Everything I do is for you. You don't see it, but one day you will. One day you will be able to see and hear my love for you. My love for you is as big and endless as the night sky."

Ehnita sighed and turned her head to look out the window. She knew her mother meant what she was saying, but she resented her for saying it all the same. For the past year she and her mother had been at a stalemate. Ehnita refused to drive up to the reservation to visit her mother, and her mother refused to leave…for any reason.

When Ehnita left the reservation when she was sixteen, she was sure that her mother would follow her, not immediately but eventually. But Oneida never did. Oneida stayed on the reservation, and she held onto the hope that one day Ehnita would return. Despite Oneida's pleading and begging her to come back, Ehnita had always felt abandoned, like she wasn't enough for her mother, and because of that, she decided to be someone else— someone better. Ehnita left the reservation when she was sixteen and entered the suburbs as Ana.

Deciding to leave the reservation wasn't difficult. She had always felt out of place, very much the stranger in a strange land. Her mother was always off visiting people Ehnita didn't know, leaving her to play with kids and interact with them in a language she did not speak within a culture she wanted no part of. When she finally left the reservation and went to make the suburbs her home, she found herself the odd girl out once again. This time she spoke the language and she knew the customs, but she didn't look the part. For Ehnita, her whole life had been about waiting to feel like she fit somewhere, waiting for someone to see her, to reach out to her. So, when her boyfriend, Ben, asked for her hand in marriage, she of course said yes.

"Mama, I'm not lonely. I have Ben."

"No, Ehnita, you are not *alone*, but *yes*, you are lonely. There is a difference. It's like the moon in the night sky; it looks alone, but it is not lonely because the moon has the whole sky. One day you will know the difference, and when that day comes, you need only touch the sky—all my love is there waiting for you. You will never be lonely again."

"Okay, Mama, I have to go now. I've got to get up early for work in the morning. But think about what I said. Whenever you're ready to get off the res, let me know."

"Okay, my child, you sleep well. And do not forget what I have said. Whenever you are ready to come home, I will be here waiting, right here between heaven and earth, waiting for you."

Chapter One

I have reviewed your response, and while I understand your trepidation, I assure you, that which is considered "sacred" can most certainly be built upon and around. I hope this week that you will allow me the opportunity to put your mind at ease. In fact, I hope it pleases you to know that in the next couple of days, I personally will be presenting your vision to the tribe of the future for the falls, a future full of prosperity, beauty, and unification.

I promise you that not only will the tribe support this vision, but they will also embrace it wholeheartedly, as I already have. They are, after all, my people. And a win for one is a win for all.

I'll be meeting with the sheriff in the coming weeks to go over our progress, of which I am confident there will be a great deal.

Until then,

Anita

"You about done?"

Ehnita studied the email curiously. She was uncertain whether she'd said what she needed to, to put the partners' minds at rest. "Yes, I believe I am. I mean, I'd believe me, but will they? I don't know. Come take a look and tell me what you think."

Ben didn't hesitate when asked; he quickly made his way from Ehnita's living room to the small office in the corner and picked up the laptop. His concern and attentiveness weren't so much about Ehnita as they were about himself. Since he and Ehnita were partners on this development project, her interests were his interests. Just as her success was his.

Ben read the email four times before setting the laptop back down on the desk. "It's good. I especially like the part about you being one of them. That was a good touch."

For the past two years, Ben and Ehnita had been the perfect couple. From the outside looking in, the two of them appeared to be equally yoked. Aside from good taste in wine, nice clothes, and expensive jewelry, the two of them also shared the same career goals and opportunistic spirit.

Ehnita took the laptop back from Ben and dragged it in front of her and gave the email one last look before hitting send. "Yeah, I thought that might help. Kind of like saying, *Don't fear the tribe. I am the tribe and if I love it, they will too.*"

"Will they?"

"Will they what?" Clearly confused, Ehnita turned to face Ben while he elaborated.

"Will they love it?"

Ehnita scoffed and shook her head as she made her way out of the office and walked into the kitchen. "How the hell should I know? I mean, seriously though, what's not to love? The building will be spectacular, the views will be epic, tourism and commerce will go up, and unemployment will go down. Seriously, what's not to love?"

The question was rhetorical, of course, but hearing it out loud, she couldn't stop herself from answering her own question. "Well, I'm sure they'll find something to complain about."

"What's that?"

"Nothing. You want a glass of wine?"

"Yeah, I'll take a glass of red." Refusing to let the moment pass, Ben stood with his arms folded, facing Ehnita, and waited for her to respond. "You said something. What did you say?"

Now, almost as annoyed with Ben as she had been with the email she resented feeling like she had to write, Ehnita rolled her eyes at Ben and quickly shoved the glass of wine into his hand.

"Nothing. Nothing important anyway. I expect a little pushback but nothing I can't handle."

"You think the tribe's going to be a problem?"

"I think all of our projects have their share of *issues*. But thankfully, I'm great at resolving issues. So, don't worry about it. I swear, you're starting to sound like one of our worried partners. I wish you'd relax."

Ben loosened his tie as he took a seat on the barstool opposite from where Ehnita stood. "It's a huge project, Ana. I've got a lot invested in this. We can't afford to have any issues at all, let alone one of this magnitude."

"I've got twice as much invested as you, and you don't know a thing about the tribe. I do. Trust me, they'll be fine."

After swallowing the wine in his glass, Ben got up and reached over and snatched the bottle of red off the counter and emptied what was left of it into his glass. Ehnita had yet to have her first glass, and Ben knew this, but the comment about her larger investment rubbed him the wrong way, and he couldn't resist taking a small jab at her. This particular bottle of red was her favorite; it was also the most expensive bottle she had. Drinking the last bit of it while she watched him gave Ben a certain satisfaction. He may not have been able to control the project's negotiations, but he could definitely control the mood that evening, and he enjoyed doing so.

"I don't know the tribe the way you know the tribe? You lived there for like a half a second, thirteen years ago; maybe you don't know the tribe the way you think you do." Ben smiled and inhaled the wine in his glass. As he slowly exhaled, he rose to his feet and raised an eyebrow at Ehnita and smiled.

From infancy until about the age of nine, Ehnita had lived in a very affluent part of Tucson with her mother and her mother's foster parents. It was just after her ninth birthday that her mother decided to return to the reservation, return to her people...to go back home. Returning home was a concept Ehnita could never fully wrap her head around because for her, she was already home, and her mother's people were strangers to her—with major emphasis on the *strange*. Despite her desire to stay where she was, they left and went back to a place that she'd never been before and lived amongst family she never took the time to get to know in the six years she was there.

Ehnita knew what she said in her letter about her relationship with the tribe wasn't what Ben was concerned about. What concerned him was her comment about their investments into the project. It was that statement that had him riled up. They'd both stopped taking on new clients to focus on this one; the money they were losing, their status in the office was on the line if things went sour. There was a lot of risk. At work they were technically classified as equals, but as far as capital and portfolio, Ehnita had Ben beat hands down—a fact that Ben hated and was working diligently to change.

"I lived there for six years, Ben. Believe me, I know what they need."

Six years had been six years too long as far as Ehnita was concerned, but legally she couldn't just leave when she wanted. Her mother was her guardian, and according to the law Ehnita was in her care until at least the age of sixteen. And as much as it pained Ehnita to be there, she refused to reenter what she considered to be the *real world* as a criminal. So, on the eve of her sixteenth birthday, at the door to the trailer she and her mother lived in, and with her bags packed and at her side, she stood there silently from eleven o'clock to midnight waiting. At twelve o'clock on the dot, she left and never went back, and she promised herself that she never would, not until she had *made something of herself.*

Once she was out of her mother's house and off the reservation, she moved back in with her mother's former foster parents and finished high school in the suburbs. From there she went on to college and graduated cum laude. It didn't take her too long after college to land a high-paying job at a company with a good reputation, and as soon as she did, she went back to the reservation to show her mother all that she had accomplished. She wanted to gloat. She wanted to show her mother everything she had earned was because she hadn't stayed. Her desire to stand face-to-face with her mother and say, *I told you so*, was so overwhelming, Ehnita nearly screamed it in Oneida's face. Despite Ehnita's accomplishments, Oneida was not impressed. The only thing her mother was truly interested in hearing about was when Ehnita would be returning home.

All the accolades and all the accomplishments that Ehnita felt were praiseworthy suddenly meant very little to her. She knew that she disappointed her mother, and with that knowledge she grew to resentment. She resented her mother for making her feel that way; she resented the reservation for the hold she felt it had over her mom. Each time Ehnita went to the reservation to visit her mother and share with her some *good news*—a promotion, a new client, a new man—she'd always leave feeling like a failure. Eventually she stopped going. And then her mom died. Suddenly, returning to the place she blamed for her loss and all her disappointments, facing people she didn't know and never tried to understand, it all felt like a waste of time.

This development project was taking her back to a place she had once sworn to never feel beneath her feet ever again.

Closing this development deal meant *going home*. It meant coming to terms with and acknowledging who she was—which was the same person she'd run away from years ago. It meant lying about having a place with a community she felt like she never fit into. But to cement her position in the place she'd adopted as her home, to finally feel as if she'd made it and earned the right to be where she was, she would have to face who she'd been saying she wasn't all her life.

"Ben, look, you don't know what it's like there. They want this. Believe me."

"Do they know they want this?"

Ehnita smiled over her shoulder as she walked to the opposite side of the kitchen to retrieve another bottle of wine. She had only three bottles left, and she didn't want to open another, but she refused to let Ben think he'd gotten the best of her that evening. She refused to let him win. As she poured herself an extra-large glass of her very expensive wine, she looked over her shoulder at Ben and smiled. "I'll convince them."

Ben knew he'd been one-upped, but he decided to let it go. "I'm sure you will."

"Cheers to that." Ehnita coyly smiled as she lifted her glass in the air toward Ben. Ehnita's biggest adrenaline boost in life came from proving people wrong, a character flaw that developed the day she left her mother's house. Her mother cautioned her not to go; she warned her that she would be lost if she left, that her life would never be full and that it would lack meaning. Determined to prove her mother wrong, Ehnita became everything that her mother, Oneida, wasn't. She became determined to go further academically, do more professionally, to have more of everything; and she pursued these goals furiously without any regard for others, without telling the entire truth, without being true to herself and who she was. She was far from the woman her mother had tried to raise her to be, but to Ehnita that was a win, because to her, her mother's life was a stereotypical tragedy.

"Okay, now that that's done and we can relax, I was thinking about sushi for dinner. What do you think?"

Ben shrugged ambivalently. As he scrolled through his phone, he could feel Ehnita staring at him, waiting for him to look up. He hated when she did that because to him it was obvious that he was listening; he didn't need to look at her to hear her. Sighing as he continued to scroll, he shrugged again. "Sounds good to me, but are you forgetting, Miss Fancy Pants, that place you love requires a reservation, and we don't have one? It'll be like a two-hour wait, at least."

"Ben, be serious. We never have reservations when we go. The owner of the sushi restaurant is one of my clients. He always finds room for me."

Ben's gaze immediately shifted from his phone to Ehnita's smug face. "Well, excuse the hell out of me. I didn't realize we were so important these days."

She'd done it again, but she knew she did it this time. Just like Ben, Ehnita was not one to back down, not even for the man she was about to marry. Him not looking at her while she was speaking annoyed her, and she knew that he knew that. So, if he wasn't willing to give her his full attention, she was more than prepared to take it; and so, she did.

"Don't be childish, Benjamin. I know the owner personally. We went to Berkley together. We knew each other before this restaurant was even a thought. This is how he shows his gratitude to me for helping him bring his dream to fruition. So yes, I've got a guaranteed table for myself and others, whenever I need."

"I know where you went to college, Ana. You don't need to remind me."

Despite growing up in privilege, Ben had not accomplished half the things Ehnita had. He was an attractive white guy—6'2" with blue eyes, blond hair, and an athletic build. He came from an affluent family who prided themselves on their family's legacy of being *the first* in America, one of the families who helped build the colonies. Ben was the *all-American boy;* he was the bar; he was what others were supposed to aspire to—good looks, charm, good family, big trust account. It irritated Ben that Ehnita didn't act humbler toward him, more grateful to be with him; it frustrated him that she didn't seem to know her place.

Ehnita went to a better university than Ben, and she got better grades and graduated with higher honors. Currently, she earned more money than he did, and her condo was twice the size of his and more expensively furnished. Ehnita made a point to show off without having to verbally say that she had what she had. It was right there in people's faces, and it was presented in such a way that you couldn't avoid seeing it.

Knowing that she was getting under his skin, without much effort on her part, Ehnita sat smugly on her barstool and slowly kicked one foot back and forth as she watched him stew. To make matters worse, her coy smile only accentuated how strikingly beautiful she was. Even if you knew nothing about her, she'd still stand out in a crowd based on her looks alone. She refined her look as much as she could so that she could fit the image of what she envisioned status to look like. Her jet-black hair was treated three to four times a month to get a high gloss shine to it, and then it was sectioned to create big, wavy curls that fell to the middle of her back. Her makeup was always high end and flawless; her high heels were always designer and never scuffed; her dresses were usually bodice; and her nails were always perfectly manicured. If the Barbie makers ever decided to do an Indigenous line, they would call Ehnita to help with the prototype. Her bronze skin glowed even through the makeup powder she pressed on her face to dull it. Her dark brown eyes sparkled like reflective pools, and she had the shape of a gymnast but with a body that possessed the softness of a flower. She was naturally stunning beneath all the beautiful she put on every day.

Loosening his tie as he leaned on the counter, Ben glanced at Ehnita before taking a sip of wine. "You know what? I almost forgot the game is on tonight. We should stay here and order in."

With her sights now set on sushi, Ehnita felt a little deflated, but she shook the feeling off quickly. "Okay, you know, that actually works out better. This way we can finally get some wedding planning done."

They'd been engaged nearly a year, but as far as wedding preparation went, there was little to nothing done.

"Do we really need to do that tonight? The game season is just starting, and I want to relax; we've been working hard all week. Don't you want to kick back and relax a little?"

"You're comparing our wedding to our job?"

"That's not what I meant, and you know it."

He hadn't gotten down on one knee, and there weren't any roses involved or mood lighting and soft music, but Ben had asked Ehnita to marry him. But from the time that he had asked for her hand up to now, whenever the subject came up, he'd quickly change the conversation.

"So, are we supposed to stay engaged forever?"

Taking a final sip from his wineglass before placing it on the counter behind him, Ben grabbed Ehnita by both arms and quickly kissed the side of her head. "Ana, you know I love you, and no, we're not going to stay engaged forever. It's just that weddings are a lot of work and planning, and we've been so busy already with this new development deal, honestly, I'm exhausted. Aren't you? As soon as this deal closes, I promise, we'll start planning things."

If Ben had been marrying anyone other than Ehnita, then everything he said would have made complete sense, but he wasn't marrying anyone else, and the only planning Ehnita had in mind was setting a date. She didn't care about caterers, venues, flowers, or all the other details that went into a wedding. All she wanted was her dress, her groom, and her marriage certificate. She had only agreed to a big wedding because it was what Ben's mother had wanted, and Ehnita figured if the woman couldn't get the daughter in-law she wanted, Ehnita would compromise and at least give her the wedding she wanted for her son.

"Okay, fine. Once The Falls project is done with, we'll sit down and plan everything then."

"Thanks, babe." Smiling as he grabbed his keys off the counter, he quickly gave Ehnita another quick kiss to the side of the head before heading for the door. "I'll see you tomorrow at the office. Get some rest."

"Wait. I thought we were ordering in. You're going home? I thought you were staying here tonight!"

"I'm gonna grab a bite to eat on my way back to my place. I've got some papers there that I have to bring to the office tomorrow, and it makes sense to leave from there instead of staying here and driving back and forth. Plus, if I leave now, I can be home before the game starts. That way I don't miss anything."

He had already missed something—which was the fact that Ehnita hadn't eaten either because she had been waiting on him, but it didn't matter, because Ben was out the door before Ehnita could respond. As the door shut, she sighed and accepted the fact that tonight, much like every other night of her life, she would have to fend for herself.

<h1 style="text-align:center">Chapter Two</h1>

Seven forty-five Monday morning, in what she called her *temporary office*, trying to establish a baseline on which all her arguments would stem from, Ehnita sat reading case law from the mid-1900s. For her, this was more than just a development project. This was her time to shine. This was vindication and validation of everything she'd been saying for as long as she could remember.

The workday had barely begun, and yet Ehnita had half a day's work already completed. Saying she was driven would be an understatement. When it came to proving a point, she was relentless and had a one-track mind.

"Morning, Ana. If you have a second, I thought I'd check in and see how things were progressing on The Falls development project." Tripp Hallowell, board member, development record setter, and all-around sleazeball, stood in front of her door with his hands in his pockets, slyly staring over at her as he awaited her reply.

Clearly confused by his intrusion but not wanting to show it, Ehnita quickly shook off the shock she knew she must have shown. She hadn't heard anyone knock on her door, and the last time she looked up, it was closed. She admired his track record at work, but she despised his hubris and his sense of entitlement. This wasn't the first time he'd shown up at her office unannounced and uninvited. Even outside of work, out for drinks, Tripp had always displayed this sense of superiority around Ehnita that she couldn't stand.

"Not running into any trouble, are you? You know, this is one of those make it or break it types of projects. I'd hate to see things go south for you. Anything I can do to help?"

Tripp wasn't a large man in any sense. He was about 5'8" and 165 pounds soaking wet, but Tripp's ego stood at 6'3", 220 pounds and was currently smothering Ehnita. Every time he saw her, he was always wanting to *check in* and offer his assistance, *wink, wink.*

"Trouble? No, no trouble at all." Ehnita smiled confidently as she leaned back in her seat and quickly crossed her legs. "I appreciate the offer, but don't worry, I've got this. In less than ninety days, we'll all be toasting to the future of the new Wyhech Falls."

"And what about Benjamin?"

"What about Benjamin?"

Slowly unbuttoning his blazer as he silently walked in her direction and took a seat on the opposite side of her desk, Tripp stared intently at Ehnita and searched her face for any disturbance, any trace of fracture or uncertainty. "Does Benjamin share your confidence about the project?"

Despite Tripp's quick rise to prominence at their firm, when it came to potential relationship suitability, he was considered to be subpar by almost every female member of staff; for Ehnita he was completely unacceptable. The fact that when she took on this project, he called her his *little Pocahontas* and patted his mouth like a big dumb idiot only solidified Ehnita's contempt for him. Not that it mattered, because he didn't seem to notice, or he didn't care. Ehnita had become somewhat of a novelty to him, a prize he had to win, a toy he wanted to take away from Ben. He used his daily project check-ins with Ehnita to *check in* on the status of her relationship as well.

Smiling, as she always did when he asked about Ben, Ehnita put her hand on her heart to really lay on the false affection. "Of course he does. In fact, Ben and I were just talking about going on vacation somewhere together after everything is finalized."

"Is that so?"

"Is what so?" Smiling as he walked into the office, Ben rubbed his hands together and confidently walked toward Ehnita and took his place behind her. Smile on his face but arms folded across his chest in defiance, Ben leaned back against the windowsill and cleared his throat as he looked down at Tripp.

With a slightly forced laugh, Tripp slowly rose to his feet and rebuttoned his blazer. "Speak of the devil."

"And he shall appear." Ben's chuckle was just as forced and short as Tripp's laugh. Both men were opportunistic little corporate climbers. Tripp had the prominence, but Ben had the girl; each wanted something the other had, and they both knew it.

As he leaned over to rub Ehnita's shoulders, Ben looked up at Tripp and smiled. "So, what was it you two were in here talking about?"

"You actually, and The Falls project. I was checking in to make sure things were running smoothly and to offer my assistance to the both of you, should you need it."

"Thanks, man, but we're good. Right, Ana?"

Ehnita smiled and nodded as she swiveled in her chair. "Absolutely. Thanks for checking in, though, Tripp. We really appreciate it."

Tripp walked out of Ehnita's office, and Ben followed behind him to shut the door.

"What the hell did he want?"

"Nothing. Just fishing around, as usual." As she reopened the file on her desk, Ehnita sighed and shook her head.

"What?"

"Nothing. I don't understand why you get so bent out of shape around him. Yes, Tripp is a scumbag, but he's also a partner. You need to learn to check your emotions a little bit better."

"Please, spare me another lecture on the art of being cold and distant. I get it. You're the queen of icy."

When it came to Tripp, Ben knew Ehnita was right, but he decided not to follow her advice; instead he did whatever he wanted to do. And what he wanted to do was the exact opposite of whatever Ehnita said. "I got a call from our buyer this morning."

"Oh yeah? About what?"

"It seems he decided to take a trip up to the Falls over the weekend to get some specs done, and he brought his architect with him."

"Did they enjoy their trip?"

"It wasn't much of a trip, actually. It seems they were met with a lot of resistance from the local tribe and were not so nicely asked to leave." Fed up with her ambivalence, Ben reached over and flipped closed the file in front of her. "Hey. They're questioning if we can get this done. They're not happy."

"Well, they shouldn't have gone up there without telling me. I could have—"

"You could have what? It's clear the Cheveopai don't want to sell. And now our buyer is questioning whether you can deliver on everything that's been promised. You said you could get the tribe to see things our way."

"I can and I will. It takes time."

"Damnit, Ana. We don't have time. Our buyer is ready to close in ninety days."

"And I'll have the Cheveopai convinced in thirty." If Ehnita was shaken, no one would know it, not even the man in front of her who she had shared her bed, her body, and the past two years of her life with. As she slowly reopened the file, Ehnita smiled and rubbed the top of Ben's clenched fist. "Ben, relax. Trust me, I've got this. *We've* got this. In ninety days, we'll both have bigger offices and healthier bank accounts."

Chapter Three

The ride from Tucson to Phoenix took up the better part of Ehnita's morning on Tuesday, but after her conversation with Ben the day before, it was a trip she felt she couldn't avoid. It wasn't that she didn't love catching up with her foster grandparents; it was that the purpose of the visit wasn't a casual meeting—it was for business. Her mission was to do as much recon as she could before she went into battle. She wanted to be armed and ready, to equip herself properly, and that meant driving to Tucson to collect things she'd previously regarded as junk.

It was almost noon by the time she drove up the driveway to the contemporary single-family home that housed the people she called *family*.

"Ana, love, it's so great to see you. Hurry up in, dear, and get out of the heat before your hair starts to frizz." Barbara stood in the doorway, beckoning Ehnita inside. Barb was as lovely as she was confusing. She hated the heat yet moved from San Francisco to Tucson. She wore white tennis skirts nearly every day of the week, but she didn't play tennis. She shopped compulsively for high-end evening wear but was always in bed before dark. She flinched at babies and never wanted children, but blathered to whoever would listen about how she almost single-handedly raised Ehnita and put her on the right track. She never let Ehnita forget the *better* life she was afforded thanks to her generosity.

"Hey, Barb. I'm coming."

Even though Barb and her husband, Martin, felt like family to Ehnita, she never referenced them as such, which was their choice, not hers. When Ehnita was five, right before she and her mother left Tucson, she'd called Barb "Grandma." Even though she was young and, since the incident had occurred, had been through many things throughout her life, she never forgot that moment. It was Ehnita's first year of kindergarten, and in school they'd made these melted crayon leaf pictures to bring home as gifts; she was so proud of the pictures she'd made for her mother and for Barb. After giving her mother her picture and being gushed over and praised for her artistic ability, she was all teed up for more praise and affection when she handed Barb her picture. "I made one for you too, Grandma."

Laughter. Hysterical laughter and some white wine spittle on her arm was what Ehnita got instead of praise. "Oh dear, no. I'm not your—Ehnita, you know you don't have to call me Grandma. You call me Barb. What's gotten into you? Grandma. Heavens no. You'll confuse people. The things people would say. It's Barb, sweetheart. Let's stick with that."

"Sorry to barge in on you like this, Barb. But this development project has been a little bit more difficult than I anticipated, and I need all the help I can get."

"Oh, you're no trouble at all, dear. Go on and sit down and relax yourself. I have the chef preparing lunch for us, and the housekeeper is in the garage now pulling that box you asked for. Now you take a seat and tell me all about it."

To a stranger, Barb, dressed in sterile white, and her home, specifically her living room with its expensive glass vases and one-of-a-kind steel lighting fixtures, would have appeared cold and vacant. But to Ehnita, it was all that she wanted and everything she strived for. This woman and her taste were what she had modeled her life around.

"Well, as it turns out, Barb, you were right about my mother's things. Thank you so much for hanging on to them for me and not throwing them out when I insisted. As it turns out all that junk might have some use."

"I told you, Ana, you never know." Barb loved being right just as much as she loved mild weather. Her satisfaction in the moment showed clearly on her face. Whatever Ehnita's problem was, it was irrelevant; her need for the items didn't matter either. The only thing that mattered was that she had been right.

"I know, you tried to tell me, but I wouldn't listen. Thank God you didn't listen to me." Apologizing and admitting wrong, for Ehnita, felt as foreign and confusing as it sounded coming out of her mouth. "I need to establish a connection with the Cheveopai, and I'm hoping there's something in all that junk that might help me do that."

"Oh, you and your mother's people."

Ehnita winced at Barb as she quickly cleared her throat. "My mother's tribe, yes. Well, their reservation happens to occupy a large portion of land where one of my clients intends to develop. The structures they want to build, Barb, they're absolutely spectacular. I've never seen anything like it. This project could turn out to be one of the best things that's ever happened to Phoenix."

"Well, that certainly sounds exciting, but it also sounds like it might not happen. Not if you're banking on your people moving off that land to make it happen."

This time, Ehnita managed to catch herself and not wince at Barb's assertion and designation of who she belonged to. Instead, she sighed and smiled slightly as she casually rubbed at the headache starting in her right eye. "Which brings me to the box."

"Oh sweetheart, I don't think any of your mother's old junk is going to help you here. I mean, you saw how she was. She was always going on about the earth and how sad she was that it was being destroyed." The memory of Ehnita's mother's sadness, something she saw as completely ridiculous, brought a frown line to Barb's forehead, one she quickly rubbed away with her finger.

"Obviously, I anticipate there might be some resistance, but I figured if I could find a point to connect with them on, I might be able to persuade them to change their minds."

"And if not? If there's nothing in your mother's box that will help you connect with them, to convince them to move, then what?"

"Then I'll find another way to convince them. Whatever it is I have to do, I'll do. It's not about what they want; it's about what's best for Phoenix, and this project going through is what is best for Phoenix. The jobs that it'll create and revenue, for not just the city but for individuals. If they don't see things my way, believe me, I can find others who will, and then the tribe will wish they had. I just don't want to go that far yet."

Both women took a sip of their lemonade and sat quietly for a moment. There was something between the two, an unspoken rivalry that had been there for so long that neither could truly tell where it began, but both of them, if they were being honest, could absolutely tell it was there.

Ehnita had always been headstrong. Who she was in competition with and trying to prove herself to, truly, Ehnita didn't even know herself; but the who and the why didn't matter to her. Ehnita had been this way for so long that she refused to change. Even if she never figured out who she was competing against, she was too afraid to see who she'd be if she weren't striving to be better than someone else.

Recognizing Ehnita's efforts was always entertaining to Barb. She took pleasure in watching others try to have the things she did, to try to establish themselves and get to the same place that she'd been born into. It amused Barb to watch anyone try, but it amused her more when it was Ehnita. She took great pleasure in watching Ehnita try and try again. Even though all that Barb had was inherited, not earned, it didn't matter to her. She had it and enjoyed watching others trying to get it.

"You seem quite determined about the matter."

"I am."

Barb raised an eyebrow almost in admiration, but the sentiment was short lived, and her mood swiftly changed direction. Her features read more *touché* and cautioned Ehnita to be on her guard. "Well then, count me in. Anything I can do to help you, let me know. In fact, I have a friend or two on the Urban Planning and Development Committee down your way. I could make a few calls on your behalf if you need."

Never in a million years would Barb have guessed that her fluke idea to take in a Native foster kid would end up like this. In reality Barb and her husband, Martin, taking in Ehnita's mom, Oneida, when her mother was younger was not at all Barb's idea. Martin was no bleeding heart either, but he was trying to win votes to become senator. He needed a platform, and taking in Oneida and her child gave him more than just one platform; it gave him three: family, diversity, and charity.

"That would be great, Barb. I'd love a chance to discuss some of the history surrounding the land with someone. There's a loophole somewhere, and I'm sure with the right background information, I can find it."

"Say no more, Ana, darling, consider it done. I'll reach out to the committee first thing in the morning." Barb sighed triumphantly as if the deal was all but sealed now that she was involved. "How wonderful it'll be to finally put up something beautiful and profitable in place of that rundown, unkempt wilderness. But enough about that. Let's go on into the dining room and have some lunch, and you can catch me up on how things are going between you and Benjamin."

Sitting in the dining room, Ehnita looked at the empty seat next to where she sat, the seat her mother had previously sat in when they lived there together, and she found herself full of regret but couldn't understand why.

"Oh, Ana, did I tell you that Claire Kinlow is married to a senator now?" Nodding in approval of her own statement as she looked down at her salad that she was cutting up, Barb smiled confidently as if she had something to do with it. "Weren't you and Claire friends? If I can recall correctly, you two were actually quite close."

Claire Kinlow, who lived down the street from Barb, had been Ehnita's first friend as well as first frenemy. In kindergarten the two shared everything with each other, but in high school the sharing stopped; it had become a relationship where Ehnita was always giving and Claire was always taking.

"Yes, Claire and I were very close. We haven't spoken in a few years, though. I guess we're both really busy. I'll have to find her number and give her a call to congratulate her."

Ehnita's statement had clearly struck a chord with Barb, who immediately put down her knife and fork and threw her hands up to feign exhaustion…exhaustion from what, Ehnita was never quite sure. "Busy is not the word, Ehnita, darling. Being the wife of a senator is absolutely exhausting. Believe me, I know firsthand."

"Of course. I can only imagine." As she sat at the table with her glass of lemonade pressed to her lips and listened to Barb go on and on about her hard knock life as a senator's wife, Ehnita's mind began to wander back to when she was sixteen and sitting at this same table, feeling much the same way she felt at this exact moment—like she didn't measure up. *Claire was busy*. Claire, who didn't have a job, was busy. In Barb's eyes, Ehnita couldn't hold a torch to Claire, and this was the way it had always been. Ehnita was nothing when looked at alongside Claire, a woman who had worked for nothing but still managed to accomplish so much in life.

It wasn't just with Barb; she'd felt this way with everyone. She was never enough; she never measured up; she was never good enough. Although her mother had never said it, Ehnita could feel it—a part of her mother felt that way about her too… She wasn't in tune enough with her roots to connect with the people she was supposed to be rooted with.

"And another thing, Ana, I saw some of Claire's wedding photos when I ran into her mother the other day." Placing one hand on her chest and holding the other out in front of her, Barb gasped. "Stunning. Absolutely stunning. Anyway, my point is that before you and Benjamin get married, you should see Claire's stylist and have her cut your hair. The curls you put in are lovely, but all that hair on your head makes you look so, so—I don't know the word I'm looking for…"

Indian. That was the word that Barb was looking for, and Ehnita knew it.

"I don't know. Your hair is so long, love. Claire's stylist did an absolutely amazing job on her. I'm sure she could do wonders for you."

When Ehnita was younger, Oneida used to hum to her as she brushed her hair. Now, as an adult, Ehnita was never more at peace than when she got out of the shower and sat in her bedroom brushing her hair with her eyes closed, listening to the memories of her mother's voice. Cutting her hair, cutting that string to the one memory that brought her so much calm wasn't an option for her. "Yeah, definitely, Barb. I'll ask her for the information when I call and congratulate her."

"Wonderful, darling. Now, I suppose the only other thing we need to focus on is your makeup and finding you the perfect gown to match that lovely skin tone of yours."

Permanent tan is what Claire used to call it. Dismayed but smiling and nodding as she looked at Barb and agreed with everything said, Ehnita silently dug her nails into her palms and tried to swallow the pain she felt on the inside. Her heart seemed to race and fracture all at the same time, and Barb, her *family,* was none the wiser.

Chapter Four

"Black Raven? Black Raven? Hello? Black Raven, could we please—"

The sun finally made its way around the clouds and through the trees as Black Raven held his fingers to his lips and inhaled the light.

"Black Raven, look, I get it. It's beautiful out here, but I think we could get much more accomplished if we went inside and sat down and talked."

"Ehnita, you and the sun are not rivaling, my precious Moon. We will stay here. It is not often you two are in the same place at the same time."

Ehnita couldn't care less about the sun overhead. She was hot, exhausted, and irritable, and hearing her name pronounced properly and in the way her mother would have said it added to her frustration. For so long she had allowed—rather, she insisted that people call her Anita or Ana for short. She almost believed that Ana was her real name.

Back in downtown Phoenix, she was Anita, sharp-minded, career-driven, independent woman, but here on the reservation, she wasn't any of those things; here under the scrutiny of the sun, Black Raven had exposed her. She was Ehnita, EH-NEE-TAH—Moon. No one here knew Ana in the same way that Ana didn't know Ehnita.

In spite of the heat, as Black Raven spoke, chills shot up and down Ehnita's spine. The last person to call her Moon was her mother. In this moment Ehnita hated her name almost as much as she hated this excursion. The saving grace with her name, however, was that no one ever knew her name had a meaning, let alone what that meaning was; it was much in the same way she didn't understand why she and Black Raven were standing in the woods that day. The purpose and meaning of this experience were lost on her.

"You know, Black Raven, if the trees over there weren't in the way, you'd get much more sunlight here. It would really open things up and make it beautiful."

"Make it beautiful?"

"Yes. Just imagine all these trees gone, a clear, unobstructed view of the sky. You'd be able to see the horizon."

"I see."

A burst of adrenaline flooded through Ehnita's veins, and she finally felt like she was making progress. He saw her vision, and he was listening to her.

"And to you, Moon, destruction is beautiful?" Black Raven shut his eyes and slowly shook his head in dismay. "This is not good. This is not who you are. How can you find beauty in destroying that which you are meant to protect?"

Deflated and a little stunned, Ehnita stammered, trying to recover and hide her disappointment. "I—I mean we wouldn't, I'm not..." Sighing as she moved closer toward Black Raven, Ehnita put on the biggest smile she could muster. "It's not destruction. We wouldn't be destroying anything; we would be making room for something better."

"Adding to something where there is no space for it doesn't make things better; it makes it crowded. It makes it different. Add too much and something gets lost. Something always gets lost."

The conversation had taken a turn in the wrong direction, but at least the conversation had finally begun, and Ehnita was thankful for that. After her lunch with Barb the day before, she had decided to stop by the reservation and smooth things over with the tribe in regard to her client's impromptu visit so that afterward she could confidently go back to her clients and reassure them that everything was on the right track.

"Black Raven, I promise you, this is a good thing. You and the people here will be lost without it. You're running out of resources here. This project can help improve the lives of everyone. It would give them revenue, stability, and an opportunity for growth."

Smiling and nodding as she spoke, Black Raven moved slowly away from the shallow stream where they stood and walked a path from memory that Ehnita struggled to follow in her red-bottom heels. "And what will this project take?"

With her mind somewhat preoccupied trying to remember exactly which store she'd gotten the Saint Laurent she was wearing from, her response to Black Raven was a little delayed.

"Come now, Moon. You must know what you would be taking. For every day there is a night; for every death there is a life; for every give there is a take. What will you take?"

"Nothing. This isn't about taking. It's about working together and accomplishing something so that everybody wins."

Black Raven sucked his teeth as he continued walking. He never slowed on his journey to accommodate Ehnita, even though he could hear her struggling to keep up. "You know better than most, Moon, *everybody* doesn't win. Someone wins and someone loses. Someone sacrifices and someone gains."

They'd finally made it to a clearing when Black Raven stopped. Ehnita's two-thousand-dollar shoes hadn't survived the journey, and neither had her hair, which was beginning to cling to the sides of her face from all the perspiration.

"Have you ever been here before, Moon?"

"No, Black Raven, I can't say that I have."

"This is the Great Falls."

Ehnita looked at the barely moist wall of rock in front of her and rolled her eyes. Years ago, the water here had run so fiercely that the people in the area said it looked like a wedding veil. But over time the water had stopped rushing. There was still water there, underground and in the streams that had been created that started at the base and led downstream to a lake. Even still, if you looked closely, you could see some of the water seeping out from various spots in the wall that once was a waterfall. She'd seen the falls from a distance before but had never been at its base; however, whether it was from a distance or right up close, she was severely underwhelmed.

"Black Raven, the waterfall has been dry for decades. Water will probably never fall from here again."

"The water falls now, Moon. It has never stopped."

Chapter Five

This evening, as was the case most Friday evenings for Ehnita, she was at home and officially off the clock, but still elbows deep in work.

"What exactly are you looking for?"

"I'll know when I find it."

"Well, maybe if you gave me a clue as to what it is you're thinking, I could be of use."

Ehnita sighed and continued to flip through the pages of the land allotment and titles book she'd taken out earlier that day. The tiny island in her kitchen was currently under siege and being overtaken with history books and entitlement law pamphlets.

In spite of his halfhearted efforts to assist, Ben was relieved to see Ehnita getting so consumed in her work. Ehnita in this moment was the woman he had fallen in love with. She was determined, fierce, unforgiving, and still someone he could easily overshadow at the same time. Ben had all the other qualities that she lacked. He had an undeniable presence about him, he was confident and charismatic, and most importantly he was widely accepted and found highly palatable in all social situations.

Books were Ehnita's *big guns,* and when she brought them out, watch out; she would loophole herself in and out of whatever quandaries came her way. She was determined, or what Ben had affectionally liked to call *savage,* that is until Ehnita made it explicitly clear that "savage" was an adjective he was never to use to describe her…ever.

"Okay, babe, well, I'll leave you to your reading. I'm going to sit in the living room and watch the game. Let me know if you need anything."

Treaty, Sovereignty, In Trust Of—page after page after page said essentially the same thing. Purchased from, held in trust of for, and it always ended with the word *Sovereign.*

After Ehnita's visit to the reservation three days ago, her time spent listening to water that wasn't there taught her one thing: She needed a backup plan. Standing there that day with Black Raven at the base of the waterfall that had been dry for decades reminded her of how she felt as a child when her mother first brought her there.

In her first weeks on the reservation, Ehnita had decided her mother was crazy, that the reservation had made her crazy. Her mother sang and flitted around their new sardine can of a trailer as if she was staying in the penthouse of the Ritz Carlton. In the blink of an eye, Ehnita had gone from a house with more bedrooms than there were people to sleep in them, to sleeping accommodations that lacked privacy and instilled in her a very real fear that their home would be hitched up in the middle of the night and towed away with them inside. And her mother—her mother couldn't have been happier. Every morning, she would beg Ehnita to come and sit outside with her and listen to the earth.

Ehnita's mother wanted her to listen to the earth that couldn't speak, and Black Raven wanted her to listen to water that had run dry. She could never reason with her mother. Where Ehnita saw opportunity, her mother saw sacrifice; where Ehnita found victory, her mother found sorrow; when Ehnita triumphed, her mother's heart broke. The two were diametrically opposed to one another's way of being. When Ehnita left the res, their differences only became that much more evident, but it never stopped Ehnita's mother from pleading with her to come home and sit outside with her and listen to the earth.

"The answer is here; I just don't see it yet."

Settled into his corner on the couch, Ben barely tilted his head in Ehnita's direction as he shouted across the room.

"What's that, babe?"

After topping off her wineglass, Ehnita went and sat next to Ben and let out a huff. "I said, the answer is staring me in the face, and I can't see it yet. I can feel it. I know it's here."

"Well, if you need me to step in and take over, let me know." His eyes were still on the television as his finger hovered on the buttons on the remote. Ben scooted back further into the corner of the couch and completely relaxed his body. "I'm here for you. We're in this together."

Despite being her partner on the project, Ben knew less about its details than some of the firm's new hires. He wasn't bad at his job, when he actually decided to do his job; however, on this task he was decidedly resigned to ride Ehnita's coattails all the way to his new corner office.

His hollow offer went through Ehnita like a cool breeze. She quickly shook off the uncomfortable feeling his insincere statement had left on her and flipped open the book she'd brought with her from the kitchen. She found herself equally discomforted by her choice in literature that evening as she was by Ben's false offer of assistance.

After flipping through the book briefly, she decided she'd clearly grabbed the wrong book from the store, because this book was all about restoration and the revitalization of a lost nation. The words *stolen, destroyed,* and *wept,* they all seemed to leap from the pages of the book and assault her eyes.

Reading was getting her nowhere. Wine in hand she made her way down the hallway to her bedroom to retrieve the box she'd picked up from Barb's house. All that she had left of her mother was in this box, and now, over a year later after her death, Ehnita was finally going to open it; she never thought she would. She'd decided when she was given the box, even without opening it, that there was nothing in it worth value to her. Why would she want anything from a woman who, she had declared on more than one occasion, had nothing to offer?

Back at the island of books in her kitchen, Ehnita set the box down and sighed as she finally opened it and took a look inside.

There weren't too many items in the box, which didn't surprise her at all, but the items that were inside made little sense to her, which slightly intrigued her. Her mother had always been a bit of a puzzle Ehnita couldn't figure out; perhaps finding the significance in her things would finally help her piece things together.

"Oh Mama, if you'd have listened to me, you could have had so much more." Ehnita sighed again and reached down in the box and pulled out a thin gold chain with a crescent moon pendant attached to it.

Legs stretched against the length of the sofa and his head resting on the armrest, Ben slightly tilted his chin forward in acknowledgment but never took his eyes off the TV screen as he feigned interest in what his partner was doing or might be saying to him.

"What was that, babe?"

Ehnita glanced in Ben's direction and quickly shook her head and smirked. Her mother definitely had not approved of Ben; however, Ehnita refused to take any kind of relationship advice from a woman who hadn't been in a relationship with anyone since Ehnita was born. She always told her mother she was going to die alone if she didn't put herself out there, but her mother would always laugh and say, "Dying alone is not an option for me."

Amongst the assorted items in the box was the handmade dream catcher that her mother had made for her when she was six. She remembered seeing it when they moved back to the reservation and asked her mother why she hadn't thrown it out. Her mother's reply: "All your dreams will always be safe with me." Also in the box, a purple calla lily pressed between wax paper, several turquoise and jade stones, a charm bracelet with Ehnita's birthstone on it, a dirty-looking flintstone suede dress with matching slippers, some old, faded papers in a language she did not speak, and lastly a picture of her mother alongside Black Raven.

"I can't believe it." Ehnita flicked at the picture and sucked her teeth.

"Believe what, babe?"

"Believe *him*."

Picture in hand, Ehnita stomped back into the living room toward Ben and handed him the photo.

"Look. It's him, the guy, Black Raven and my mom."

"Who the hell is Black Raven?"

Ehnita had forgotten she hadn't discussed in detail the events of her trip to the reservation. "He's the man I met with when I went to the reservation. He's what you would call a *medicine man* of sorts. Anyway, he never mentioned knowing my mother. Don't you think that's odd? They look pretty close in this picture."

"You think he might be your dad?"

Feeling a bit assaulted by the question, Ehnita leaned back to shake off the sting she felt on her cheeks. "My father? No. Why would you say that? What would make you say that?"

Realizing how upset she'd gotten, Ben muted the television and looked down at the picture one more time before handing it back to her.

"I'm just saying, you never met your father. Your mother never spoke about him. Now you meet a man who knew your mother but doesn't speak about her. And like you said, they do look pretty close in the photo."

Ehnita looked at the picture again. It was the happiest she could ever remember seeing her mother. The people in the photo were more than close; there was something shared between them, a feeling between the two that Ehnita could not put her finger on. Her mother stood facing Black Raven, her head tilted up to him and her eyes filled with so much light, they seemed to dance. And his smile was so pure and sincere, Ehnita could feel his joy as if she were there herself. With his fingers at her mother's chin and her mother's hand pressed to his chest, it was as if the camera had captured the two sharing a secret.

"He's not my father. I would know if he was."

"How would you know? The place for your father's name on your birth certificate is blank."

"I would know, okay?"

Ben chuckled as he picked up the remote and unmuted the television. "*You would know*—maybe you're more Native than I thought."

"And what is that supposed to mean?"

Ben's education in Indigenous people, despite the fact that he was about to marry an Indigenous person, was elementary at best. When he thought of Ingenious his thoughts went to cowboys and Indians, witch doctors, half-dressed men riding wild horses, and a host of other dramatized stereotypes.

"Nothing, babe." Still chuckling to himself, he put his feet up on the coffee table and aimed the remote at the TV and huffed to himself. "*Just know…* Sure you would."

Chapter Six

"Sheriff, thank you for coming down. I know you must have a lot to do, and I appreciate you taking the time."

Sheriff Wes Tonka was a stocky, medium-sized man with chestnut-colored skin and thick, shiny black hair, which he kept pulled back into a low ponytail.

"No problem at all, little sister. Everything is quiet back at the res. If making a trip to you means keeping those guys off our land and keeping them from upsetting people, then I'd gladly make the trip anytime."

Ehnita forced a smile and smoothed the nonexistent wrinkles from her form-fitting pink structured dress. She found herself oddly relieved by the sheriff's presence. He wasn't at all what she was expecting.

"Yes, the developer. I am so sorry about that. I wish he would have told me he wanted to visit; I would have absolutely called you first to make the proper arrangements."

As far as the men involved on this project went, Wes seemed like he'd be a much more pliable person to deal with. She was by no means above using her feminine wiles to get what she wanted, and the sheriff was single, older, and seemed to have an interest in her. She preferred accomplishing things based on her wit rather than her wiles, but she could do the damsel in distress route if she had to. She was more than willing to take any advantage she could get as long as it got her the result she wanted in the end.

"Please, please, Sheriff, have a seat. Can I get you anything? Tea? Water?"

"Oh no, thank you very much, I'm okay." As he sat, he placed his hand over his heart and bowed his head slightly in respect. "So, how is it I can help you, sister?"

Ehnita smiled but it annoyed her to no end that he kept calling her his sister. She was not his sister; he didn't even know her. That Monday morning was the first time she'd ever laid eyes on him. They'd spoken on the phone previously, but it was always business. They weren't even friends; she most certainly had no intentions of recognizing him as her family, but for the sake of negotiations, she decided to let it go and not mention it regardless of how much it irritated her.

"Well, I'm not sure if you were aware, Sheriff, but I was up at the reservation a few days ago."

"Yes, I am aware. You went to meet with Black Raven."

Pausing, she plastered on another fake smile. "Yes, of course you are. Being the sheriff and all, you must keep track of who comes and goes."

"Not really." Shrugging his shoulders ever so slightly, he tilted his head and put his fist up to his mouth, quickly clearing his throat. "What I mean is, yes, I keep track but not because I'm the sheriff. I keep track because we all keep track. It's what we do. We keep track of each other, watch over one another. You know how it is."

"Of course," she lied. "I know exactly what you mean." Softly folding her arms as she rested them on her desk, Ehnita laced her fingers together as she quickly reassessed what she wanted out of today's meeting. Initially, she wanted an ally, but now above all else she wanted information.

"Sheriff Tonka, how long have you known Black Raven?"

"All my life."

"So he's lived on the reservation for a while then?"

Clearly confused, Wes hesitated as he considered his response. "Yes, all his life he has lived on the reservation."

"What is it exactly that he does there? When I first called you and asked for a referral, someone I could discuss planning with, you referred me to him. Why? What does Black Raven do on the reservation or for the reservation? Why refer me to him?"

The more questions Ehnita asked, the more confused Wes became. "What do you mean, little sister? Black Raven is an elder."

"Oh, okay. And that means he does what, exactly?"

"It's not *what* he does; it is *who* he is."

Sensing that her questions were beginning to leave a sour taste in Wes's mouth, Ehnita took a breath and decided to do something she rarely did. "I'm sorry, Sheriff. I didn't mean that the way it came out. Let me explain myself. I understand that he's an elder and that elders are respected. But what I don't understand is—and this may be because I left the reservation a long time ago— why is he referred to for business decisions, especially on topics he may not have any knowledge in. Wouldn't it be wiser to rest the future of the reservation, the health and financial well-being and progression forward… Would the people of the tribe not be better served by someone, say, someone like you, for instance?"

"Me?"

"Yes, you. You've gone to college, you've got a good job, you communicate with people on and off the reservation. Why not you?"

In that instance, Ehnita's previous assessment that Wes was kind and gentle was being challenged. All the previous softness his face had when he first stepped into her office had gone. His cheekbones seemed more defined, and his brown eyes seemed darker and sharper than they had been before.

Ehnita quickly straightened up in her chair and placed her still folded hands gently in her lap.

Wes took his right fist and placed it over the middle of his chest. "Sister, I would never insult an elder, especially Black Raven, by trying to take their place in the community and speaking for them. That is not our way."

Finally realizing the offense she caused, Ehnita took a breath and relaxed herself.

"Oh no, Sheriff. I didn't mean to imply that you would ever do such a thing. I thought it would be more practical having someone who speaks with both sides involved in the project is all. Forgive me. I never meant that I thought you should replace Black Raven." Manipulation hadn't worked, but her ability to bend the truth was still on point. Replacing Black Raven with the sheriff was exactly what she wanted.

"It's okay, sister. No apologies necessary. I misunderstood. The fault is mine." With the softness returned to his eyes and the coldness gone from his face, Wes also relaxed and fell back into the amenable mood he was in previously. "Also, sister, we already have someone that speaks to both sides. We have you."

Ehnita was stunned. She had never considered herself as part of the reservation or a member of the tribe, no matter what she put in that email she sent to her boss.

"But, Sheriff, I represent the developer on this project. I can't speak for the tribe too."

"Isn't that what you're already doing? You speak to us of the developer, and you speak to the developer of us. See—both sides."

Being unable to say what she truly felt left Ehnita speechless. As she sat there with her contoured face and lip-plumping matte lipstick and all of the other daily essentials she put on so as to look nothing like the man sitting across from her, the man who insisted on calling her family, she assumed he'd be able to tell just by looking at her that she in no way wanted to be considered part of the tribe. The tribe's interest was not her interest.

"Sheriff, I would be happy to continue to be the go-between. Perhaps we can do a town hall meeting or something to get everyone together. I can lay everything out for the community and then they can raise any concerns they might have."

Slowly rising to his feet, Wes nodded in agreement. "Yes, that sounds good. Next time you meet with Black Raven, you should bring that up and see what he thinks."

Seeing him nod had given Ehnita a jolt. Ideas raced through her head as she rose from her chair, but upon hearing Black Raven's name once again, she tripped over her own excitement while making her way around her desk to see Wes out the door.

"Black Raven, yes, I will definitely mention it to him the next time I see him." Since they were still on friendly ground, Ehnita decided to take the opportunity to get some personal information out of today's meeting, especially since she knew she wouldn't be getting anything else. "You know what? I found a picture of Black Raven with my mother's things. I had no idea they knew each other. Did you know my mother, Sheriff? Do you know if she and Black Raven were close?"

Joy spread over Wes's face so pure and so sincere, it was almost childlike. "Yes. Yes."

Before she could follow up on his statement, there was a quick tap at her slowly opening door. "Hey, babe. I heard you had company."

Ben opened the door wider than he should have and bumped Wes with the knob. Instead of apologizing, he simply slid through the opening and made his way over to Ehnita's side.

Gone again was the friendly face that Ehnita hoped would help her seal the deal on the development project and solve the mystery of picture.

"Sheriff Tonka, this is my fiancé, Benjamin Pierce."

As Ben began to extend his hand, Wes quickly flicked the brim of his hat and gave a sharp nod to Ben before turning around and grabbing the door.

"Good to meet you, sir. Sister, I will let Black Raven know to be expecting you."

"Goodbye, Sheriff. Thank you again for making the time." Frustrated, Ehnita drew back the fingers on her hand and slowly let her head fall in disappointment. "Damn it."

"Not the friendliest guy, is he?" Ben plopped down in the chair previously occupied by Wes and scrolled through his phone, casually humming to himself.

Frustrated and annoyed, Ehnita shut her door and walked back over to her seat. "*Yes. Yes.* What does that even mean?"

Ben frowned as he peered up from his phone. "What does what mean?"

"Nothing. It doesn't matter." Ehnita quickly waved off Ben's inquiry and exhaled her irritation. "What did you need, Ben?"

"Need? Nothing. I came in to help."

"And how exactly did you plan on doing that?"

In a very childlike manner, Ben threw his arms in the air and looked at Ehnita in disbelief. "Did you not say how important family and community are to these people? I came in to show him that. To show him how everyone working on the project here is family. We're all on the same team trying to get the same thing. If he hadn't left the way he did, I could have gotten that across to him."

After some thought, Ehnita decided that Ben was right. "Thank you, Ben. You gave me a great idea."

"You're welcome. You wanna let me in on what this great idea is? Like I said, Ana, we're a team, and so far, our team is down on the scoreboard. If you need me to step in, I wish you would say—"

"I've got this, Ben. And if the tribe isn't responding to me and I'm native born, what makes you think they'd respond to you?"

With a huff, Ben returned to scrolling through his phone. "You say that like you're one of them, but everything about you says you're not. Including you. At least I wouldn't be insulting them by pretending, little Miss Native for Negotiations."

Chapter Seven

A few days had passed since Ehnita's meeting with Wes, and as she drove through the reservation on Sunday morning, she looked around at the scattered homes along the main street and sighed. To her, they all looked sad and ugly. The homes' exterior paint was faded and dirty, and the porches were cluttered with items she assumed were trash. "This place is begging for a makeover."

Ehnita chuckled to herself as she continued to drive. "I finally heard the earth, Mama. It said, *Get this crap off me.*"

Still very much amused with herself as she walked into the sheriff's office, which was tiny, Ehnita was smiling ear to ear. Wes, not realizing that the source of Ehnita's joy came from less than kind thoughts she had about the community he loved, he smiled back.

"Little sister, so good to see you again."

Before Ehnita even had a chance to say hello, Wes was out from behind his desk and standing in the doorway with his arms open, ready to embrace her as he welcomed her in.

Startled by the affection, Ehnita let out a nervous laugh. "Oh, hi there. Good to see you again too."

After pulling out a chair so that she could sit down, Wes quickly turned to the table in the corner of his office behind his desk where there lay plates covered in tinfoil. He fixed Ehnita a small plate of berries and cake and poured her a cup of mint iced tea. "Please, eat, relax. You had a long drive."

The pound cake looked as if it had gotten stuck in the tin it was baked in, and the tea was the darkest she'd ever seen.

"Thank you, Sheriff."

With his hand raised, halting her, he smiled. "Wes. Please, call me Wes."

"Okay then, Wes." Pleasantly surprised, Ehnita smiled and nodded. She had already decided that Wes's first name was something like Little Foot or Big Bear, despite the fact that she had lived on the reservation when she was younger and remembered knowing other children there with names like Laura, Marie, and Joseph. Her adult mind played to stereotypes—not quite as badly as Ben's mind did, but it was negative all the same. Wes was not at all the name she was expecting, and she found herself pleasantly surprised and grateful for his name's simplicity. She strongly disliked when animals or objects were given as names for people; she thought it was silly. The irony of the situation, however, was not lost on her. How could it be with a name like the one she had… Moon.

"Thank you, Wes. I hope my stopping in doesn't bother you. You're always so kind to me, I didn't want to park in your parking lot and not stop in and say hello."

"You're no bother at all, sister. It's always a pleasure to see you. It's always a good thing when family returns home, right?"

Ehnita smiled and nodded. That was exactly how had she felt when she left the reservation and went back to live with Tripp and Barb—it was a good thing.

While she had no intentions of eating and chatting the day away with Wes, she didn't want to be rude either, so she popped a few berries in her mouth and pushed around some pieces of cake. "I thought Black Raven might be here by now. You think he forgot about me?"

"Black Raven, forget you? Never. That would never happen. He's probably sitting on his porch waiting for you now."

"Waiting for me on his porch?"

"Yes. You remember the way to his cabin, right?"

"I think so." Annoyed that she'd have to trek downhill to Black Raven's cabin on foot, since the path was not car accessible, it added to the already ill feelings she had about the meeting. The only positive she found in the situation was that she was able to put down the snack plate Wes had given her and cut short the small talk.

"Wow, I didn't realize. I thought he would have met me up here like he did the first time I came up." As she grabbed her purse and made her way to the door, Ehnita shrugged. "I better get going. I don't want to keep him waiting."

Outside, behind the sheriff's office, Ehnita looked at the path that led to the woods and she sighed. "Another pair of red bottoms bites the dust." Inhaling deeply as she made peace with the fact that she'd likely be parting with yet another pair of shoes, Ehnita slowly exhaled the hot air that had been filling her cheeks and took her first step forward.

She hated this hike the first time, and she hated it even more the second time around. It was barely noon, and she was already in a sweat. Her silk blouse clung to her back like sticky honeycomb, the curls in her hair began to fall and frizz, and ringlets clung to the sides of her face, obstructing her view. It was as if the trees, the sun, and her hair had conspired to blind her that morning.

Finally, almost twenty minutes after she first began her trip down the path, she arrived at a clearing and could see Black Raven's cabin ahead. The cabin was small, miniature in fact when comparing it to the landscape that surrounded it. The faded brown wood exterior blended against the wooded background seamlessly. The branches and vines that grew up the sides of the house seemed as if they were holding it in place and keeping it protected. The plank stairs that led to the porch reminded Ehnita of the steps to her mother's home, where she refused to sit when she was younger.

As she paused to take a breath, Ehnita looked out in front of her past the cabin. She could see clearly all the space that she hadn't known was there that could become her client's. In her mind she was putting up buildings and roads everywhere. The thought of bringing the developer's imagination to life reinvigorated her, and she quickly wiped the sweat from her brow and moved toward the cabin with her chin held high.

"Good morning, or should I say afternoon?" A little winded but still uplifted by previous visions in her head, Ehnita smiled and waved as she approached.

"Good afternoon to you."

"Sorry to have kept you waiting, but I thought I was meeting you at the sheriff's office. My mistake. But I'm here now. I made it."

Black Raven looked out into the land behind Ehnita, as if he was seeing right through her. "Yes, you did. I see you."

"And here you are. Right on your porch, just like Wes said you'd be."

"Where else would I be?"

The sheriff's office came to Ehnita's mind, but of course she decided to keep that thought to herself. "Where else indeed. Well, should we step inside now so that we can get started?"

Ehnita stood by the front door, ready to open it, but Black Raven never moved an inch.

"Why do we need to go inside? There is a chair there in the corner. You can bring it over." He never turned his head or averted his gaze from the woods in front of him; he only gently lifted his arm and pointed in the direction the chair was located. "Join me, Moon."

Not wanting to start the conversation off on a bad note, as reluctant as she was about having a meeting outside, she went and retrieved the chair without protest.

After she settled into the uncomfortable wicker chair, she confidently placed her purse on her lap and began pulling out laminated graphs and plans she'd brought with her to truly give him an idea of what the developer had envisioned.

"I brought these to show you. I think maybe last time I was here, I wasn't able to give you the full picture on things. So, I thought what better way was there to show you than to bring these."

Ehnita held the diagrams with the tips of her fingers toward him, but he never even twitched in her direction.

"The full picture is right here in front of you, Moon."

Ehnita glared at the woods. "Black Raven, please, would you just look at the diagrams? I truly think you'll be surprised. The land has so much more to offer than I even thought. The possibilities and opportunities are amazing. This development project could do a lot of good for a lot of people. If you would please give me a chance to show you."

Black Raven took the diagrams and quietly studied them. He went over each outlined proposed structure with the tips of his fingers, slightly shaking his head as he went.

"What's wrong? What are you saying no to?" Ehnita sat on the edge of her seat, ready to defend the work and to tear down any objection he might have.

"All of it."

"All of it? You don't like any of it?" In disbelief, she shifted in her seat and tried to calm herself. "Okay, well, how about you tell me what it is exactly you don't like about it, and we can try to work from there."

As he handed back the diagrams, he sighed. "Oh, Moon. There is nothing to work on. You cannot see what is already here, so how can I tell you? But don't worry, you will see. I will show you."

Feeling as if she'd been cut off at the knees, Ehnita huffed as she slapped the diagrams down in her lap.

"Show me what, exactly? I can see already what this place means to you. I'm not trying to be insensitive, but I can see what this place is now, and I can also see the potential it has, and I'm excited about it. If you would just give me a chance—"

"And I will, Moon. As long as you promise to do the same."

"I promise." Ehnita spat the words out before she truly knew what she was signing up for. "What do you need me to do?"

"Come back."

"*Come back*? That's all?"

"Come back and learn and truly see the land. Once you can clearly see what is here, then we will try to figure out how to make what you see fit into this vision."

"Done."

Black Raven laughed and reached for his pipe. As he lit it, he chuckled to himself before inhaling smoke and silence. When he exhaled, he looked at the large smoke clouds and grinned as if they shared some secret in that silent moment. "As long as they get their way, the young are always eager to try a new way of doing things." Another inhale and seconds later thunderclouds of smoke rolled out of Black Raven's mouth and clung to the sky. "*Kariwase.*"

"Kariwase?"

"Yes. Kariwase. A new way of doing things. A new way for both you and I."

Chapter Eight

She could never understand why, but it always felt as if the fancier the restaurant, the less full she felt by the end of the evening—regardless of how much the meal cost.

The dining room was gorgeous, and the restaurant was unquestionably fancy, except in her mind it wasn't the type of place one came to eat. She equated the restaurant to an elegant dress you couldn't sit in, but you just had to have, and you wore it anyway because it looked good, and at the end of the day—looks mattered.

"What I don't understand is what you're going to be up there doing. And what am I supposed to tell the partners? You want me to tell them that you're sightseeing?"

Ben groaned as he looked up at the ceiling and ran his fingers through his hair in frustration. "Our client was already nervous, Ana; this does not help."

Ehnita knew Ben was right, but she had no intention of telling him so. Instead, she rolled her eyes and gently laid her napkin across her lap. "Ben, I said before that I could get this done and I will. I mean seriously, how worried can the partners be? They handpicked us for this project out of all the people in the firm more senior than us. They knew we could get it done. They need to trust their initial instincts. I've got this."

"*You've* got this. This is not a one-person project, Ana. This is my name on the line here too. You cutting me out of the planning process doesn't help matters."

"Yes, I know it's *our* project, and I'm not cutting you out. Your style doesn't work or add anything at this stage, so let me handle it. Seriously, the only thing that matters is that we get them to sign. It doesn't matter who convinces them as long as they're convinced."

She wasn't sure when it happened, but around the office, somehow, she and Ben had become somewhat of a package deal. Sure, they were getting married, but both had worked for the firm longer than they'd been together as a couple. Between the two of them, and in spite of Ehnita's track record of success, it was Ben who was more on track at becoming a partner than she was. Ehnita had been with the firm five years longer than Ben; she worked three times harder and had ten times the success rate. But none of that seemed to matter much to her superiors because in the end, Ben still somehow outranked her. Over time, Ben somehow managed to become the face in front of all of Ehnita's hard work.

When The Falls project presented itself, it was the first time the partners had picked Ehnita to be the face of something she worked on; however, she had been chosen not for her detailed work but for the details in her face, her heritage…which meant nothing to her personally, but it meant everything to the project.

The land in question had been sought after before, highly desired by many developers, but the Cheveopai would never sell. Offers that other people would hope their entire lives to see never enticed the tribe. But things were different now. The Cheveopai population had grown over the years, and their resources had not. Instead of a grocery store, the Cheveopai had gardens; instead of tarred roads, they had rocks. Instead of picturesque views, they had a dry waterfall. They needed more resources to sustain their growing numbers. And what better person to tell them this than someone who looked like them.

The new dynamic didn't suit Ben, so he decided not to follow it. His halfhearted attempts to be the brains behind the face were short lived, but he wasn't completely removed from all the work. He knew what he could gain from the project's success, so he stayed as minimally involved in it as he could.

"What does your mother want to see us for anyway?"

"Don't call her that, Ben. You know she hates that."

"Fine then, your *Barb*. What does your Barb want to meet with us for anyway?"

Ehnita truly wasn't sure; neither did she care. She was always excited when Barb called, which was hardly ever. It was usually Ehnita calling her.

"I'm not sure. She said she wanted us to meet someone."

"Uh-oh, is she leaving Martin?"

"Don't be ridiculous. She'd never do that."

While Ehnita's mother had never met Ben, *her Barb* had. Barb gushed over Ben the first time they met. She went on and on about how lucky Ehnita was to land a man like Ben. Ben reveled in all the praise and enjoyed spending time with someone who he felt could recognize his worth without having to be told to do so. Barb and Ben were two people cut from the same cloth. They got along so well that Ehnita felt like an intruder whenever they got together; it was almost like they had a club amongst the two of them, and she was standing at the door, waiting for one or the other to look up and invite her in.

As predicted, Barb walked up to the table decked out in all white. Today it was a classic Chanel suit with matching purse and hat and a pair of lambskin Balenciaga pumps. Ehnita tugged at the sides of her perfectly fitted canary-yellow Calvin Klein dress and felt inferior.

Ehnita rose to her feet despite Barb's halfhearted protest. "Barb, it's so good to see you. How was your drive?"

After exchanging an air kiss to the sides of each other's cheeks, Barb laughed and gave Ehnita a soft swat to her arm. "Don't be silly, dear. Drive? Oh no, I called a car service."

Of course, you did is what crossed Ehnita's mind as she smiled back at Barb. Still smiling as widely as she could manage, Ehnita turned to Barb's guest, who had been not so subtly admiring her figure. "Hi, I'm Ana and this is my fiancé, Ben."

Hand extended toward Ben, but eyes still on Ehnita, Bill nodded to himself as he clucked his tongue and smiled.

"Nice to meet you, Ana, and you too, Ben. I'm Bill Rathers."

Ben straightened his blazer before shaking hands with Bill and then made his way around to schmooze with Barb. "Mrs. Barb, you are as stunning as ever this evening."

"Oh, Benjamin, you flirt. If I wasn't happily married, I'd give Ana here a run for her money over you."

Once they were all seated and everyone had ordered, Barb, per usual, took control of the table.

"Ana, Benjamin, Bill is a former senator from Tucson. I've told him about your little tribe situation, and he thought he might be able to give you some advice and direction."

"Absolutely." Ben took a sip of his martini and sat up in his chair. "This is perfect. Ana and I were just discussing other possible avenues to take to push this deal through."

Barb smiled at Ehnita and winked before turning her attention back to Bill.

"Well, in my experience the tribes have always been extremely temperamental and territorial when it comes to any kind of discussion about *their* land. Now, why they'd rather see good land go to waste and have their people struggle has always been beyond me." Bill took a quick sip of his gin and popped a piece of bread in his mouth. "It's not like anyone's trying to trick them or take anything from them. From what I hear, your offer sounds like it would be a win for them."

Ehnita nodded as she scooted forward. "That's exactly what I've been trying to tell them."

Barb flashed Ehnita a quick look from the corner of her eye. After her silent scolding she looked down at her salad and smiled away her contempt and disapproval of Ehnita for her interruption.

"I believe you have, sweetheart, but I think you're approaching it the wrong way."

As Bill stuffed more bread in his mouth, Ben put down his glass and leaned into the table. "What do you mean, *the wrong way?*"

After washing down his bread with the rest of his gin, Bill wiped his mouth and slowly taped his finger on the table. "Now,

I believe if you address the individual instead of the group, you would be more successful."

"Yes, I probably would. But the tribe does not work like that. They function as a whole." Ehnita may not have known much about the people she so closely resembled, but she knew that much.

"Yes, but if you really look at the tribe, they're not that different than any other community. You're always going to have your *haves* and your *have nots*. You need to find out which of the deed holders are your have nots. Dig into their lives, their financials, their extracurriculars. Find out exactly what it is they don't have and then give them some of that."

Ben was now on the edge of his seat. Telling people what they wanted to hear and getting them to take something he'd convinced them they needed was his department. When it came to negotiating contracts and dealing with the legality of things and paying high attention to detail, that was Ehnita's department. Ehnita was the hammer and Ben was the feather, but now this was his opportunity to stop floating around and waiting for Ehnita to get things done. In a situation like the one that Bill was suggesting, Ben could finally be the hammer. He could be the one to fix everything.

"That seems totally doable. Make it look like they never lost anything at all. Show them what they'd be losing if they stayed." Ben smiled wide. "I like it."

"Exactly." Bill reached for his newly topped-off glass of gin and took a sip. "You only need two or three families to sign and then boom, you've got it all. The rest won't stay if they know you're coming."

"That's brilliant, Bill. I knew you were the right person to call." Barb grinned from ear to ear, more pleased with herself than she was with anything Bill had said that evening.

"Yes, Bill, thank you so much for your advice. It's a direction we hadn't yet tried." Ehnita wasn't being completely dishonest in her response. She hadn't tried that direction because she knew it wouldn't work; her own mother was a testament to that fact. Despite all the opportunities her mother was given, she died alone with nothing, on the land that she loved, and in her heart, Ehnita knew if she could do it all over again, Oneida would make the same choice again.

Now that business was out of the way, their dinner orders had arrived at the table, and the atmosphere became a little more casual, Barb redirected her attention to Ben.

"Benjamin, my love, I feel I haven't seen you in ages. I've missed you. How have you been?"

Smiling coyly back at Barb, Ben shrugged. "You know me, Barb, just keeping busy working and taking care of my girl over here."

Grinning from ear to ear, Barb looked at Ben with a look of admiration and pride. It was a look that Ehnita envied and loathed all at the same time.

"Bill, you know Benjamin here is quite the rising star at his firm. If anyone can push this deal through, it's him."

Nodding in approval as he sipped his scotch, Bill winked back at Barb.

"Well, I appreciate your confidence in Barb." Ben didn't even look in Ehnita's direction as he accepted Barb's praise for work he hadn't even done. "I'm optimistic about the project and everything that will come from it."

"Well, you must try not to work too hard, Benjamin. Between this deal and your wedding, you'll end up wearing yourself out. So, tell me, how is the wedding planning going?"

Ehnita, very curious herself to hear his response, raised an eyebrow at Ben. In truth, Ben had invested zero interest and energy into the wedding planning at all. If things had been left to him, the two of them would have been on a permanent engagement.

"Well, you know how it is, Barb. Mom wants one thing and Ana wants another. I give my input here and there when I can."

For the first time since the conversation had started, Barb finally turned her attention to Ehnita. "Ana, please tell me that you haven't been arguing with Benjamin's mother?"

Blindsided, Ehnita coughed and tried to clear her throat. "No. Absolutely not." To argue, the two women would have to speak, and Ben's mother barely acknowledged Ehnita's existence despite all of her best efforts. Ehnita sent Ben's parents gifts on Christmas, cards on their birthdays, and champagne on their anniversary.

"Glad to hear that, Ana, darling. I'm sure Benjamin's mother just wants to help. He is, after all, her only child. She wants to make sure things go smoothly." With her well-manicured French tip nails, Barb placed the very tip of her fingers on top of Ehnita's hand. "Come to think of it, sweetheart, Benjamin's mother probably has more planning to do for this wedding than you do. I mean, the invitations and seating arrangements—I don't see how you would be able to help her with that. There won't be anyone there from your side of the family."

As both men cleared their throats and the subject quickly changed, Barb's attention once again went back to Ben and Bill. She was so busy chatting with Bill and fawning over Ben that she hadn't noticed that her last comment had hit Ehnita so hard, she had practically doubled over on top of the table as she grabbed at her stomach and tried to reach for the knife that Barb had just plunged into her.

Chapter Nine

"Since when do you work out?"

After staring for a few brief moments completely confused by what he was seeing, Ben lost interest. As intrigued as he had been initially, he didn't bother to stick around and wait for Ehnita to answer his question. Before she had even looked up and made eye contact with him, Ben was halfway down the hall and on his way to the kitchen.

"Since me *seeing* the reservation requires more cardio in a day than I normally do in a month. I've ruined two pairs of shoes already. I refuse to lose a third."

With a box of assorted K-Cups in hand, Ben stomped back to the bedroom and stood in the doorway, looking at Ehnita in disbelief.

"You're going back to the reservation? Seriously? I thought we had a new plan, a good plan, a better plan than the one you had. A plan that, by the way, did not include you listening to some pipe-smoking hermit who lives in some shack in the woods."

After giving the tongue to her sneakers one final adjustment, Ehnita plopped down on the bed and sighed. It didn't matter what Ben thought because she knew better. She knew that Black Raven was more than what Ben thought he was…so much more.

"Your plan won't work, Ben."

"And why is that, Ana?"

"It's a community. The tribe is a community, and unless you're in that community, they're not going to listen to you. They don't know you and they don't trust you. Divide and conquer will not work."

"And how exactly would you know that?"

Offended by the query, which felt much more like an attack, Ehnita snatched the K-Cup box from Ben's hands and pushed past him and headed toward the kitchen.

"What's your problem this morning? I thought you'd be thrilled we had another option to try to close this deal. Bill had a great idea; I think we should go with it."

In her heart, Ehnita knew she was right, but in her head, it was Ben who made more sense. Unsure of which annoyed her more, Ben's logic or her inability to verbalize what she internally knew to be the truth, Ehnita leaned back on the counter and silently sipped her coffee.

"Listen, instead of wasting your time and energy following some guy around the woods, you should be here, researching and strategizing. Play to your strengths. Stop trying to please people you don't even understand."

"I understand plenty, Ben. What you need to understand is that your plan will not work. Even if I could single out the ones in need, that doesn't help us if we don't know what it is they want. They could very well look at your deal with the fancy house and decide you have nothing to offer. Then what?"

In that moment, sitting on a stool across from her, Ben seemed at a loss for words. It hadn't been his experience that people didn't want something he had.

Ehnita put on her boutique jogging pants and pulled her ponytail through the hole in her matching hat. "I've got this, Ben. If it takes for me to go on a couple of hikes, share a pipe, or even kiss a baby, then that's what I'll do."

"Morning, Wes."

"Good morning, sister. How are you?"

"I'm good, thank you."

"You certainly look like you're prepared for a long day of hiking with Black Raven."

Ehnita smiled as she rubbed the fabric of her leggings on her thighs. "Yes, I am. I learned the hard way, Italian leather and river rocks do not mix."

After agreeing to disagree with Ben earlier, Ehnita drove to the reservation with a single thought in mind. *What do they want?* As she drove down the quiet streets to the sheriff's office to park her car, she looked around and made a mental list: *new house, playground, landscaping.* Everything she thought of, while needed, was all trivial and she knew it. The longer she thought about it, the louder and more singular the thought became. *What do you want, Mama?* She knew if she could figure out the answer to that question, then the deal would be done. But Ehnita could never figure out what her mother wanted when Oneida was alive and she was telling her what she wanted, so the likelihood of her figuring things out now was pretty slim. But she wasn't a quitter, and she knew it would take more than a car ride to figure out her mother, so she decided that while she was there, and Black Raven was showing her around, she would take the opportunity to point out what wasn't there and what this deal could bring to the community.

"So, where is Black Raven taking you today?"

Much to Ehnita's surprise, Wes always looked genuinely pleased to see her. Just as before, as soon as she stepped into his office, he stood up and came around his desk to hug her and pull out her seat; and before returning to his chair, without question or hesitation he placed a plate of fruit and cake in front of her along with a cup of mint tea.

"I'm not sure, actually. He didn't say."

"Hopefully he'll bring you to Auntie Layla's house later this afternoon. I know she would love to see you. Her son just had a baby, and she's having a celebration for him later."

Excited over the prospect of potentially meeting with some people from the reservation other than Black Raven and Wes, Ehnita felt a small adrenaline rush. Sadly, the feeling quickly dissipated as she looked down at herself and decided that she was not properly dressed for a party or any kind of social occasion where she wanted to make a good impression. Workout clothes and minimal makeup, she wouldn't dare embarrass herself making introductions in this state.

"Aren't baby showers only for family and friends? I wouldn't want to intrude."

After giving a quick wave and shake of the head, Wes reached for a pen. "Here's the address in case you guys finish early and you want to stop by on your own. And it's not really a baby shower; there's no gifts or anything like that. It's everyone coming over to see the baby and the family and to celebrate. There will be a lot of good food. Auntie Layla is a very good cook."

"Thank you, Wes. I'll check in with Black Raven and see what he has planned for us today, and then I'll make my plans from there."

The gentleman that he was, Wes got up from his seat and gave Ehnita another hug before walking her to the door.

"Okay, sister, I hope to see you later."

As she made her way down the trail and through the woods that led to Black Raven's cabin, Ehnita gave herself an internal lecture for not thinking ahead and packing extra clothes to meet people in.

Mildly out of breath and brow damp from the early stages of perspiration, Ehnita smiled and waved at Black Raven, who sat calmly in his rocker on his porch. If he hadn't told her to meet him there, she would have sworn she was disturbing him. He appeared to be resting rather than ready to give a tour.

"Good morning, Moon."

"Good morning, Black Raven." Instead of sitting in the chair next to Black Raven, the same chair that she'd dragged over to him the last time she was there, she let her hands rest on the back of the chair as she looked down at the old man. "So, what's on the agenda today?"

"Agenda? No agenda today, Moon. There is just today."

"But I thought you were going to start showing me around? Make me see what's really here."

Black Raven didn't respond. Instead, he extended his arm in her direction and with his palm over the empty chair, he tapped down on the vacant space.

Annoyed by not dissuaded, Ehnita sat down. "Have you changed your mind? Because, you know, Wes told me there's a party later that we're invited to at his aunt Layla's. I could run into town quickly and pick up something to change into, and we could do that instead, if you want."

"*His* aunt Layla." Black Raven chuckled. "Why would you have to change? You are fine the way you are. Why would you have to be different?"

"Oh. No one said anything, I wouldn't want to offend anyone by showing up so underdressed and with no makeup on and make a bad impression. I don't actually know Layla's son, and I'd hate to show up unannounced, with no gift, looking like I just rolled out of bed and have people thinking I didn't care."

Black Raven frowned as he tapped his fingers on the armrest of his chair. "I do not understand this trying to impress people you do not know with a face that is not yours and therefore cannot be remembered."

Not truly understanding his point, Ehnita sighed and leaned back against the chair. "So, it's no to the party then?"

"We will see Layla and the baby later, of course. After."

"After what?"

"After we start our journey today."

"And where are we journeying to?"

Black Raven laughed as he rose from his chair and slowly made his way down the steps from the porch. Ehnita didn't ask any other questions. She quickly got up and fell into step behind him.

For a while they walked along the side of the stream in silence. Today she was prepared, and her endurance was up, and Ehnita took pride in her ability to keep up with the old man. Today Ehnita walked one step behind Black Raven the entire time. While physically she was making progress and was proud of that, mentally she was stalled, and agitation was beginning to set in. Uncertain of their destination, Ehnita's tolerance for Black Raven's seeming aloofness was beginning to wear thin.

"Where exactly are we going?"

"We are already here, Moon."

Ehnita stopped and rested her hands on her hips as she looked up at the sky. "Already where? I thought you were going to show me something—something other than trees and a stream and rocks."

Now ten paces ahead Black Raven stopped and turned to face her. "That is all you have seen?" Smiling, he looked over the stream to the other side and took a deep breath.

"Yes, that is all that I have seen, because that is all that's here."

"You are wrong, Moon."

"Well, what did I miss? What else is here?"

"Life. So much life."

While she hadn't actually seen any wildlife, she was sure it was there somewhere, lurking in shadows, hiding behind the trees.

"The animals, of course. I can assure you, we've thought about the animals as well. Our goal is to—"

"Who said anything about animals?" Smiling as he turned, he resumed his pace, and Ehnita fell into step behind him.

"If not the animals, what life are you speaking of?"

"The souls of all of those around you."

"The dead?"

"The living."

"There's no one here but us." The idea that Ben had been right and she was indeed wasting her time made every nerve in her body twitch with irritation.

Back at the base of what used to be a roaring waterfall, Black Raven placed his hand on the moist and water-beaten wall and chuckled.

The way he looked as he touched the wall reminded Ehnita of her mother. In that moment she could see her mother's face clearly and hear her pleading with her to listen to the earth.

"How well did you know my mother?"

With his eyes closed and hand still resting on the wall, he nodded and grinned. "Very well, Moon. Very well."

"I found a picture of the two of you in a box of her things. You looked like you were really close."

"We were."

It wasn't the progress she intended to make, but it was progress nonetheless, and she wanted to know more.

"So, how did you two meet? When did you meet? When she moved back to the reservation? Because I don't remember seeing you when I was here, or did you guys find one another after I left?"

"I have known your mother her whole life, from her first breath until her last."

Stung by the statement and surprised by the feeling of jealousy that washed over her, Ehnita sat down on a slab of rock.

"Were you with my mother when she died?"

"Yes. I was with her, as I have always been."

It wasn't until this very moment that Ehnita wanted to know more about what happened when her mother passed away. When she got the call of her mother's passing, it had been the morning following her actual death, and when she asked what had happened, she was told that Oneida's heart gave out. Despite the fact that to her knowledge, her mother didn't have heart problems, Ehnita never looked into it. She took what she was told as truth, and she left it alone. And besides, it wouldn't have changed anything. Dead was dead; the how and the why didn't change the end result. It didn't change that her mother was gone. How she felt about her mother's death—her feelings had yet to make themselves known to her. She could say the words "My mother is dead," but she couldn't feel them.

"Well, if you were with my mother when she died, why didn't you call me?"

Black Raven let his hand fall from the rock and hang by his side. "Why were you not there?"

Offended by the question, Ehnita quickly got to her feet and tried to pull the anger she felt inside out of her by grabbing two handfuls of her ponytail and pulling it tighter.

"How was I supposed to know that she was dying? She never told me she was sick. I would have been here if she had told me.

I would have tried to help. She never said anything. How was I supposed to know?"

"You know in the same way a mother knows her child's cry. The same way that child she once carried inside of her knows its mother's heartbeat."

Ehnita had no argument. She stood there with her shoulders slumped and eyes cast downward. He had left her speechless. Just standing there was all she could do.

Making his way back to the trail as he moved around Ehnita, Black Raven gave her a gentle tap on the shoulder and a sympathetic nod.

"Come now, Moon. Now we go to Layla's to see new life."

Chapter Ten

Whether she was at home or in her office working, Ehnita refused to relent. Trying to figure out the mysteries of her mother was not helping her, so she chose to push aside what her mother may have wanted and instead focus on what she, herself, needed. Four days after her last visit to the reservation, Ehnita decided she needed more than just a friend on the inside; she needed facts.

Work life and home life had blurred into one. She'd managed to change her clothes and her scenery each day, but her mindset stayed the same. This evening at home in her cashmere jogging suit, with her hair slicked back into a tight ponytail, Ehnita sat at her desk in her leather high-back chair and stared at the mess before her. Her desk was laden with pile upon pile of papers and books. There were deeds separated by decades and sorted alphabetically; there were books with sticky note tabs of various colors marking pages to return to; and then there was her own personal list that she made on her dull yellow legal pad. To the left of her were the families she knew would never speak to her, those who would never consider her offer in a million years, and to the right, the smaller list that didn't even meet the middle of the page. They were the possibles, the maybes.

From what she could see, every family on the reservation owned the land where they lived outright. They owned it and they passed it down from one generation to the next, but they never sold it. Even those who had left the community never sold what they inherited, even if there was no immediate family to speak of.

There was always a distant aunt or cousin of sorts. However the land was passed down, it was never passed out of the community.

"Babe?"

"In here."

Still in his work clothes, Ben stepped into the small office and sat on the bookshelf that was pushed against the wall.

"What are you doing?"

Ehnita didn't bother to look his way or stop looking through the stack of papers in front of her. She hadn't told Ben about what happened on her last visit to the reservation, and he hadn't asked. She felt as if he was waiting for her to say, *you were right*, just so he could say, *I told you so.*

Despite the hollow feeling in her chest after she left the reservation, not to mention the uneasiness and awkwardness she felt, Ehnita still knew that she was right, not Ben.

"Let's go out and grab something to eat. I could really go for a good steak."

"Yeah, sure. Give me a few minutes."

Not wanting to wait, Ben got up off the bookshelf and made his way over to Ehnita and stood behind her with his hands in his pockets as he peered down at the papers in her hand.

"Well, well, well. What do we have here? Going over some ownership paperwork, I see."

Ehnita sighed. "Not to do things your way but to see where I should be investing my time while I'm up there."

"So, you're going back—again?"

"Yes, I'm going back. Black Raven still has a lot he wants to show me, and there's a lot of people I still need to meet."

"And how many people have you met, exactly? Aside from this Black Raven guy."

"Several, actually. I attended a party while I was there last Saturday. There was quite a number of people there."

"Any of them interested in the offer?"

"I don't know. It never came up."

Annoyed, Ben took his hands out of his pockets and banged them on the top of the back rest where Ehnita sat. "How did it not come up? That's the whole reason you went up there."

"It was a baby shower, Ben. Not the appropriate time to be discussing business."

Certain she wouldn't get the time she needed to finish what she was doing, Ehnita put the papers down. "I'm going to my room to change and then we can go."

Forty-five minutes later Ehnita was once again in new clothes and sitting in new surroundings, but once again, her mind was where she had left it…back at work. Despite dating and working together, Ehnita had barely seen Ben all day, so when the opportunity presented itself for the two of them to spend time together, she took it. She was there with him that evening physically, but her mind was miles way. Work was the only thing she could think of.

"What were you working on all day?"

Ben shrugged as he stabbed at the salad in front of him. "Nothing too big. Closed out a couple of accounts, met with a new client; nothing major."

"What new client?"

"Some big shot French restaurateur wanting to build a space downtown." Spotting his steak on its way to him, Ben excitedly took a sip of his martini and straightened his fork and knife in front of him in anticipation. "I have been waiting for this all afternoon."

"I thought the partners didn't want us to be taking on any new clients until The Falls project was finalized?"

Ben shrugged as he cut off a piece of his perfectly seared New York strip. "I guess they knew I could handle it."

In that moment, Ehnita was as disgusted with Ben's comment as she was with the salad she ordered. She was hungry but couldn't shake the comment Ben made to her just a few weeks back. Despite her small frame, while out to dinner with some colleagues, Ben obnoxiously mentioned to her in front of everyone at the table, "You might want to lay off all that meat and potatoes if you want to keep wearing those little mini dresses of yours." But his comment this evening, as hungry as she was, had soured her stomach.

"What the hell is that supposed to mean? Now I suddenly can't handle more than one client at a time?"

"It is a big project, Ana. Billions of dollars are on the line. The partners don't want you to get distracted."

"We're partners on the reservation project, Ben. The same rules for me should apply to you."

"And they would if you would let me help you. You keep your office door shut all day; you take off on these solo field trips when you feel like it without discussing it with me. What do you expect me to do all day, sit around waiting for you to call?"

"Is that what you've been telling the partners?" Completely blindsided by what she'd just heard, to say that she felt betrayed would be an understatement. "What have you been saying, Ben?"

Knife and fork down and hands raised in defense, Ben flashed his best *don't be mad* smile. "Look, the partners came to me on Monday and asked for an update on the project. They wanted to visually see the progress we had been making. I had nothing to give them, Ana. I guess Tripp may have filled in the others the day after he and I had lunch together."

"And now you're friends with Tripp?"

"He's a partner, Ana. And as it turns out, he's actually a pretty cool guy. We've been hanging out some, you know, going over cases and clients, talking about sports and stuff. He asked if he could help with The Falls project, and I let him know that things were moving a little slower than we wanted right now, but that we were working on it. He must have told the other partners, and that's probably why they approached me."

"So, you threw me under the bus?"

Ben leaned back in his seat and shook his head before taking another sip of his martini. "I did not throw you under the bus. I explained to them that considering the sensitive nature of this project and how much money was at stake that we had decided *together* to try an alternative tactic for our negotiations. Look, I explained how we wanted to take a gentle approach. However, if that gentle approach doesn't pan out, we've got a plan B all set and ready to go."

"And in the meantime, you're taking new clients?"

"I didn't throw you under the bus, Ana. They wanted an update. What was I supposed to tell them?"

"You could have called me, and I could have told them that—"

"Told them what? That you went to a baby shower?"

It was the truth, but it was also insulting. "It wasn't just a baby shower. It was a celebration of life. You wouldn't understand."

In truth Ben wouldn't have understood, but the hidden truth was, neither did Ehnita. When Ehnita and Black Raven got to Layla's house that afternoon, she wasn't surprised to find herself the only one there in workout clothes. Despite how embarrassed and uncomfortable she was, no one else seemed to care or even notice.

That afternoon at Layla's, Ehnita felt completely out of place; she felt as if she was ten years old again and new to the reservation. No one asked her why she was there; what they asked was if she was hungry, if she was thirsty, if she wanted to hold the baby, if she had met cousin so and so and auntie and uncle this and that. They asked her if she had been well and if she was happy. They treated her like she was family and as if it had only been a few weeks since the last time they'd seen each other.

She didn't hold the baby, and her stomach was too nervous to be hungry. Also, her mother was an only child, so she had no uncles, cousins, or aunts to speak of, so she felt somewhat awkward calling anyone anything other than their name.

At some point in the whirlwind of plates being passed, hugs being exchanged, and children whizzing in and out the door, Ehnita looked up and Black Raven was gone. He'd left her there, and once she realized it, she left too. She learned nothing, she proposed nothing, and she walked away with nothing.

"What I know, Ben, is that my plan will work. It's already working."

"Is it? That explains why you were looking through all those deeds this evening then."

Dinner had essentially ended when the conversation did. Ben ate the last bit of his steak and smiled as his last comment lingered in the air. After they left the restaurant, Ben dropped Ehnita off at her condo and decided that he'd go home to his own place that evening.

Once back inside her condo, Ehnita changed into her cashmere jogging outfit, poured herself a glass of wine, and went back to her office. Tonight, she felt a lot like she did last Saturday—empty and hollow. The hunger inside her that evening was about something more than just food. Her entire body was craving something that she couldn't quite identify.

Sipping her wine as she paced around her office mumbling to herself, Ehnita couldn't seem to keep one thought out of her mind: The same question plagued her and repeated in her head over and over again. *What do you want, Mama?*

Chapter Eleven

Unfazed by Ben's lack of confidence in her, Ehnita decided not to go into the office on Friday. Her time would be better spent out at the reservation. She hadn't seen Ben since Wednesday night. When she went to look for him on Thursday at the office, she was advised by one of their colleagues that he was in the field with his new client; it was a trip he had failed to mention, and so she felt completely vindicated in not telling him that she'd be in the field all day Friday.

This Friday, unlike last Saturday, she prepared herself for whatever curveballs Black Raven might try to throw at her while they went on their sightseeing tour. Instead of workout clothes, she wore a pair of lightweight, wide-leg, tan linen pants paired with a pink silk camisole. Instead of running shoes, she wore a pair of camel-colored sandals. And although the ponytail helped keep her hair out of her face, it was still very long, and in the heat it wouldn't stay slicked back the way she wanted, so today she had it all rolled up and pinned tightly to the top of her head in a very neat bun. She'd even gone out and purchased a completely new supply of makeup, all waterproof, smudge-resistant products. Today she was ready for a long hike, a baby shower, or even an early dinner.

When she pulled up to the sheriff's office, Wes was making his way up the stairs to the front door. When he saw her car, he stopped and waited for her.

"Good morning, sister. How are you today?"

"I'm well, thank you for asking. How 'bout yourself?"

As usual, as soon as Ehnita made it to the top of the step where Wes stood waiting, he opened his arms and embraced her.

"I'm good, sister. Very good. Thank you."

Once she was seated inside Wes's office, mint tea in hand, Ehnita looked down at the small plate in front of her and tried not to frown. There were no berries or cake. Today all Wes had to offer was mint tea and fry bread. She hated fry bread. It wasn't so much the taste that bothered her but the nostalgia that came with each bite that she couldn't swallow. Fry bread was her mother's favorite snack; it was Oneida's go-to, grab-and-go snack for her days of sitting out on the porch while she listened to the earth. In that moment as she looked down at the fry bread in front of her, Ehnita longed for the burnt cake and berries that she'd become accustomed to. At least they didn't come with memories that she couldn't bear to stomach.

Ehnita sat quietly for a moment while she flicked at the fry bread on her plate. The sound of metal banging snatched her from her thoughts and sent goose bumps up her arms. Wes was in the corner of his office, opening and closing cabinet drawers as he mumbled to himself and shook his head in frustration.

"I hope I'm not interrupting your work. I know you're just getting in. I wanted to say hello, but if you're busy, I can stop by on my way out."

"Oh no, I'm not busy. I have something here for you from Auntie Layla; that's where I was just now, by the way. Her sink backed up and I went by to fix it. Oh, she said she was sorry she missed you on your way out the other night. She would have loved to have spent more time with you."

"You are quite the Jack of all trades, I see. Sheriff and handyman." Ehnita smiled and raised an eyebrow at Wes as she watched him bow his head humbly in return. "Oh, and please tell Layla I will try and stop by again as soon as I have some time."

Wes nodded and smiled. "Yeah, I try and help out where I can, especially for Auntie Layla. She does so much for me. She's always bringing me food and making sure to check in on me, and she even visits my dad every day since he can't get out anymore."

Ehnita was genuinely surprised. When they met, she saw Layla as this small, fragile-looking elderly woman—a woman who she assumed spent her days sitting in a rocking chair and taking unplanned naps throughout the day. "Wow, Ms. Layla sure does do a lot, a lot more than I would have guessed. And she gave you something for me?"

"Yeah." Wes retrieved a small, worn manilla envelope from the cabinet. "Yes, here it is. She said it was your mother's."

From inside the envelope Ehnita retrieved a turquoise ring with a stone set in a silver band and a pair of turquoise and opal earrings. All the pieces had been cut into the shape of a crescent moon.

"Is she sure these belonged to my mother? I've never seen them before."

"Yeah. She said your mother had given them to her a while ago, and she thought you might like to have them."

Ehnita shook her head and quickly put the items back in the envelope, extending it back toward Wes. "Oh no, I can't. If my mother gave them to her, she should have them."

Wes shook his head and interlocked his fingers as he placed his hands on his desk. "No, sister, she wants you to have them. Besides, your mother was always helping out other people, donating things here, lending things there; she did it so often, you never knew which was which, and your mother never said. She always gave. It made no difference to her if she got anything back or not. But Auntie Layla is certain your mother would have wanted you to have these pieces."

Ehnita reached back in the envelope and pulled out the jewelry. After slipping the ring on her finger, she stuck out her hand and assessed how it looked. She thought about keeping the ring and passing it off as a vintage item she picked up from a little boutique whose name she would of course not remember; the earrings, however, were definitely not her style, but she tried them on anyway.

"They fit you perfectly. You look great."

Ehnita had a feeling Wes would have said that regardless of how she looked. After fumbling around the bottom of her purse, Ehnita pulled out her cell phone and flipped open the camera to take a glance at herself.

"No, not bad at all." She was pleasantly surprised how well the earrings fit her face. Even though she looked good in them, she knew she would never wear them again.

"Okay, well, Wes, I'm gonna get going now, but I'll stop by before I leave to say goodbye."

"Okay, I'll see you then."

Another hug and then Ehnita was out the door and on her way down the trail that led to Black Raven's cabin. Once she arrived, she was surprised to find that Black Raven was not sitting on the porch as she expected he would have been.

Right in the middle of second-guessing her decision to arrive unannounced, she spotted him coming from across the river, which was much wider than it was deep. Black Raven nodded at Ehnita and smiled.

"Your mother's earrings."

Touching her ears quickly, Ehnita nodded. She had already completely forgotten she had them in. "Yes, Ms. Layla returned them to me. How did you know they belonged to my mother?"

"Because I gave them to her."

Standing there in front of her, his pants soaked up to the knees, Black Raven looked back at Ehnita with a sense of longing she didn't understand.

"Come now, Moon."

He'd already walked right past her and was at least three feet ahead, but even with his back turned to her, she could still see it—the longing…it was in every step he took, every swing of his arm; a heavy, deep-seated longing that she could sense but not understand.

"Where are we off to today?"

"Today we see where the river leads us."

She hadn't expected him to answer the question, and the answer he gave was definitely not the one she thought he'd give.

She already knew where the river led. It led to a tiny lake about three miles down from where they were standing now.

Much to her surprise the direction Black Raven was headed in was not the one she knew would lead her to the lake. The trail they were currently on would take them back to the sheriff's office.

"Isn't the lake the other way?"

"Who said anything about a lake, Moon?"

"Well, you said where the water leads us. I assumed you meant—"

"Never assume. Never look for alternative meaning in an answer because you don't understand what you've been told."

She was somewhat offended by the remark but decided not to pursue it any further.

"So, you gave my mother these earrings? Were they a birthday gift?"

"No."

"Why did you give them to her?"

"I wanted her to have them."

His calm, matter-of-fact disposition annoyed Ehnita. He never went into detail. No matter how many times she led him to the water, she could never get him to drink.

Once they'd made it to the top of the trail behind the sheriff's office, Black Raven headed toward another path only five feet away from the path Ehnita had regularly taken to get down to his cabin, but this path was one she hadn't even noticed before. Once she got closer, she could see why she hadn't noticed it; unlike the trail she usually took, this one wasn't very clear. It was surrounded by overgrown vegetation and hanging branches and overall looked very uninviting.

"And where does this lead?"

"To the water."

"But we were just at the water. Is there another stream or lake back here somewhere?"

She quickly ran over the building plans in her head but couldn't recall any other water outlet being there. This, of course, did not mean there wasn't one, and the idea that she would have more opportunities to offer her client brought a smile to her face. This would be something the developer would love to hear.

"To the other side, Moon. We are going to the other side of where we were."

The deflation she felt translated into her steps. They were almost walking side by side when she thought there might be another water source, another surprise to delight her clients, but now knowing she was wrong, she once again found herself three paces behind. A few more moments of walking in silence and finally Ehnita could see a clearing ahead at the end of the overgrown path.

"Wow." Ehnita took a deep breath as she looked out over the rock cliff from where they stood. "This is gorgeous."

"Now you are starting to see. Come; I will show you more."

The view from above the stream was breathtaking. The water below sparkled in the sunlight, and everything appeared crisp and untouched. The brilliantly green trees seemed to touch the clear blue sky.

"Is this safe?" Looking at the old worn railing of the wooden bridge in front of her, Ehnita was skeptical.

"Of course it is."

Black Raven led the way across the bridge, not only because he knew the way but because Ehnita did not share his confidence in the structure. Nonetheless, once he'd gotten a good five steps in, she followed behind him.

Safely on the other side, Ehnita took another deep breath and looked around the wooded area. The air seemed different here. It was as if she could taste it.

"Now we go down to the water."

Black Raven turned and smiled at Ehnita before moving forward. It appeared to her that now, each step he took was more determined than the last. She also noticed that while he always appeared extremely calm and laid back, there was a certain peace about him and added joy that filled each and every one of his steps.

"Does anyone live over on this side? It looks like a wonderful area to live in. It's nice and quiet and away from everything."

"Yes."

Unsure if he was agreeing with her or answering her question, Ehnita shrugged and shook her head as she reached into her bag to grab her phone so she could take some pictures.

"Damn it. I left my phone in Wes's office."

"He will keep it safe for you."

"I'm sure he will. I don't like being without it."

"Why not?"

Confused as to why he would ask her such a question, Ehnita frowned. "Well, what if there's an emergency? Everyone should have a phone for just in case."

"What kind of emergency?"

"I don't know, a work emergency, or what if Barb or Ben were trying to reach me for something? Anything, I suppose."

"*Anything*?"

Feeling as if she were being judged, she gently twisted the turquoise ring on her finger. "Black Raven, can I ask you something?"

"You can ask me anything."

Squinting her eyes in uncertainty as to whether his response was sincere or if it was a dig, Ehnita hesitated but then quickly gathered her nerves and shook off the uneasiness that was creeping up her spine.

"If you and my mother were so close, why didn't we ever meet? I don't remember seeing you when I lived here."

"You never saw many things when you were here, Moon. Many things you still do not see."

Maybe he was right. Maybe they had met when she lived here, and she didn't remember. She was so focused on leaving when she arrived, she barely did anything except study and plan her exit.

"Okay. But why didn't you call me when my mother died?"

"Call you for what?"

"Because that's what people do when someone they love has passed away. You call their family, and you offer your condolences. You check on them and see how they're doing, ask if they need anything."

"These are things that you do?"

Ehnita had never had to do anything she mentioned. Her mother was her only blood relation that she knew of, and her other family, Barb and Tripp, were alive and well. She'd sent flowers and fruit baskets to clients who'd lost relatives, but she, personally, outside of her mother, had never made a call or been in the position to receive one before.

"Yes, I have— Well, I mean, I would." Frustrated with herself for making the previous statement, she now felt silly and irrational. Somehow for whatever the reason, she always ended up feeling completely nonsensical around Black Raven.

With his pipe tucked into the side of his lips and his head slightly raised, Black Raven looked down at her and studied her with raised eyebrows as puffs of smoke hung in the air and surrounded them.

"Why then did you not call me when your mother died? You did not check on me to see how I was doing."

Once again, she was blindsided. Standing there by the side of the stream, across the water from where Black Raven's cabin sat, the air felt cold and misty. With her hand pressed against the opening of a shallow cave that she had stepped into but couldn't quite see around, she sighed.

"Did you say, *check on you*? Why would I check on you? She was *my* mother."

In this particular moment, Ehnita felt as if she'd taken one too many sly insults. She was genuinely offended by the suggestion that she should have reached out to him. She turned her back on him and stared deeply into the darkness and made the decision that she would not apologize this time. She would not smooth things over.

Black Raven chuckled from outside the cave. As he leaned against the opening to the cave, he pressed his hand to the wet rock and lowered his head and smiled.

"Yes, Moon, she was your mother, but she was my family too. Married to my son. She was my daughter for many years. I am your father's father."

Chapter Twelve

Stunned into breathlessness, Ehnita grabbed at the jagged interior of the cave. As she shuffled her feet around in the darkness, she nearly lost her footing on the uneven rock beneath her. Finally, she managed to regain her balance and turned toward the opening of the cave and found the sunlight she'd been searching for.

"My father's father? You're my grandfather—"

In the entrance of the cave, there was no one there.

"Black Raven? Hello?"

But there was no response. The only sound she could hear was the soft echo of her own voice.

"Black Raven? Black Raven, where are you? You can't just say something like that and then run away. What do you mean you're my father's father? Black Raven?"

Black Raven was gone, and in his place, there was only silence and sunlight. As she stumbled out of the cave with Black Raven's last statement still at the forefront of her mind, Ehnita scanned the area in front of her, breathless, anxious, and confused; her eyes jumped from one spot to the next and then the next and the next, but Black Raven was nowhere to be found.

"Black Raven!"

Birds fluttered from the treetops that surrounded the area, their chirps the only response to Ehnita's call. Desperate for more answers and unnerved by the desire to find him, Ehnita shut her eyes and tried to steady her breathing and calm her racing heart.

The distant singing of birds combined with the sound of rushing water, along with the mist falling on her head and shoulders, helped to lower Ehnita's internal hysteria. The newfound calm, however, was quickly replaced by confusion.

"What the hell? What the hell is going on?"

In a moment of clarity, Ehnita realized she was now facing a rushing waterfall. The presence of the water confused her more than Black Raven's disappearance. A slight sense of terror ran through her veins as she slowly backed away from the waterfall.

"I—I don't… Black Raven? Black Raven, where are you?"

As beautiful as it was, the water terrified Ehnita, and she quickly put as much space as she could between herself and it. She found her way back to the narrow trail, and while it was less frightening than the waterfall, it, too, was something that it wasn't just moments ago. The trail on which she stood was not the same trail that brought her to where she was, but it was the only trail that was there.

Ehnita looked across the water and tried to spot Black Raven's cabin. Perhaps he went home. Perhaps he changed his mind about spending time with her that day, and he wanted to go home and be alone.

Across the water there was no cabin. There was barely a clearing. There was no one and nothing there at all. As she slowly backed into the bushes behind her, Ehnita searched the area, trying to find something familiar, something that could help her make sense of the situation. But all she could see were trees and sky and water.

She had never considered herself to be a ridiculous person, and she certainly wasn't about to concede to the notion that the world had somehow changed in the blink of an eye.

Determined to get back to Black Raven's cabin and let him know how not funny she thought this situation was, Ehnita turned toward the wooded area and began making her way up to where the bridge was…or should have been.

After almost an hour of walking and tripping through brush and over rocks, she found herself farther away from the falls but no closer to the bridge. Tired, annoyed, and hungry, she took a seat on the ground at the base of a large white fir tree.

"Damnit! Damnit, damnit, damnit, damnit. Damnit!"

Inside her purse there was nothing, nothing that would help her in this situation anyway. No phone, no food, no directions, nothing. And as she looked up at the sky, she could see the afternoon sun was slowly making its way west.

Out of nowhere but welcomed all the same was a sudden disturbance to the silence. Somewhere near her she could hear the sound of footsteps approaching.

"Hello? Black Raven?" Now on her feet again, clarity set in, and she realized screaming into a forest she couldn't see was probably not a good idea. Before she could make the decision to run, she found herself standing in an unfamiliar shadow.

"Hi. I'm Ehnita. I was here with Black Raven, but we got separated. I didn't mean to disturb you. But since I have, have you seen him? You know, Black Raven, I mean? You haven't seen him, have you?"

Stepping around the tree matter-of-fact, with his eyes set intently on Ehnita and his lips pressed firmly together, the man offered the one thing that Ehnita had zero interest in...more silence. More silence was not what Ehnita wanted or needed.

"Hello? Did you hear me? I'm looking for Black Raven. Have you seen him?"

Standing there in front of her, bare chested and barefoot with only a pair of mud-stained suede pants on as his dress, he stood silent and completely unbothered by Ehnita's urgent pleading.

"No."

After another moment of studying her, he slowly turned and began to walk away.

Despite having answered her question, Ehnita found his response rude. A one-word answer was in no way a suitable response.

"Wait! Could you please wait a minute? I need to get back to the bridge that leads to the sheriff's office. Could you show me how to get back to the trail?"

Ehnita's pleading did little to deter him from the path that he was already on, and she stumbled and struggled trying to keep up with him.

"Hello, I'm talking to you. Could you please stop?"

She hadn't meant to yell, not that it did much of anything. Still she was immediately sorry that she had. Halted by her own screams, standing there biting her lip in penance of her inappropriateness, she wrung her hands together and tried to figure out how exactly she was going to get assistance from the man walking away from her.

"Please—I'm sorry. I don't mean to yell. I just—I'm... I want to go home. I've been here for a while now, walking around in circles, and I still don't know where I am. I want to go home. Please. Please, help me get home."

"I do not know what office you speak of."

He hadn't turned around, but he had stopped walking, which allowed Ehnita to catch up.

"The sheriff's office. It's on the other side of the bridge."

Finally, side by side, Ehnita looked up and could see his face clearly for the first time. His presence wasn't overbearing, yet she felt tiny standing so close to him. Her five-foot-seven, petite frame seemed that much smaller when in the direct presence of his broad-shouldered, six-foot-two, muscular build. But his face was stern without being menacing. His thick, jet-black eyebrows and long lashes stood out sharply against his sun-kissed chestnut skin.

He was unlike any man Ehnita had ever met before. He was attractive without effort. His waist-length hair seemed to add to his masculinity, and his body bore a strength that no gym could have produced, He was gorgeous, and he didn't seem to know it, or if he did, he didn't care.

As he looked down at Ehnita, she quickly brushed her cheeks and straightened her back, but he seemed more annoyed and puzzled by her presence than he was interested in her beauty, which was a first for her. Men had almost always found her attractive, and she invested a great deal in her looks to keep it that way. Realizing the man looking at her now didn't see any of the things that other men typically did made her feel embarrassed, and she quickly dropped her head and cast her eyes down to the ground.

Glancing over his shoulder as he searched the woods behind them, the man looked down at Ehnita once more and silently stared at her until she looked back up at him again. "I know nothing of that either. There is no *sheriff* here."

"The nearest house then so I can make a phone call. I left my phone in Wes's office. Maybe if I call it, he'll answer."

"These things you are asking for, I have heard of none of them. Why are you here?"

"Why am I—" Annoyed and somewhat defeated, Ehnita threw her hands up in the air as she kicked at the dirt in front of her. "*Why am I here*? Good question… I don't know. I honestly don't know anymore. I thought I was here, that I was chosen, because I'm good at my job. No—scratch that, because I'm *great* at my job. But clearly I was wrong. They picked me because who else in their right mind would be out here doing this—whatever *this* is. *Why am I here*? Not a clue."

Confused by her outburst, which explained nothing, he looked down at her, studying her face carefully. After finding nothing there that could answer his question, he inhaled deeply before continuing on his course.

"Wait. Where are you going?" Quickly falling into step behind him, determined not to be left behind, Ehnita tried to compose herself. "I'm sorry I went off like that. I'm frustrated and tired, which, I know, is no excuse. I'm sorry, truly I am. Please forgive me."

"Yes."

"Yes? Thank you."

"You are welcome."

The way he spoke to her, the rhythm of his speech and the tactfulness of his statements, he reminded her of Black Raven.

"I'm Ehnita, by the way. You are?"

"Oteitani."

"Oteitani. Okay. Do you live here on the reservation?"

Ehnita's question hung in the air unanswered. She didn't bother to ask again. It was clear he had heard her, and while she found his non-responsiveness rude, she also understood it. It was a silly question; why else would he be there if he didn't live there?

Two miles in and away from the base of the waterfall, Ehnita could finally hear signs of life ahead. Her chest filled with anticipation, and her eyes stretched wide with relief. It took every ounce of restraint in her not to push Oteitani to the side and run ahead of him. When they finally arrived at the clearing, she was glad that she had hung back.

"What the hell is this?"

Chapter Thirteen

"Su—wee—"

Oteitani's call was like a crack of lightning in Ehnita's ears as she stared at the community in front of her in disbelief. She'd seen teepees before, but not like this. There were also animal skins stretched over wood and fish being cooked over an open fire and toddlers running around naked. Ehnita gasped at the sight. Anger rose inside of her and rolled around in her gut. *What kind of parents in this day and age would let their kids do that?*

The smell of the fish, which was skewered through the mouth with what looked like a tree branch, made her stomach grumble. She was hungry, but her inner voice told her it wasn't elegant enough. If she was going to eat fish, it needed to be rolled in seaweed with some sticky rice. This was all too rustic. This was beneath her.

"Is there some kind of festival going on?"

Confusion filled Oteitani's furrowed brow, and he briefly glanced down at Ehnita. As they walked through the community, each person they passed greeted him with a smile and what Ehnita could only assume was a kind word since she didn't understand the words being spoken. But she had heard them before; she recognized them as the same words that had always brought a smile to her mother's face.

Not too far from the large, open fire where the fish was being cooked, Oteitani opened the flap to a decently sized teepee and waited silently for Ehnita to enter.

Inside the teepee various animal hides covered the ground. The air was smoky and warm and smelled of meat and earth. On a pallet of multicolored hides sat the source of all the smokiness. Dressed in tan suede, with hair that looked a lot like her own before she curled it up, of course, smoking a pipe quietly by himself was the man Ehnita sensed she'd been brought to answer to.

"Sit."

Her initial response to Oteitani's command was defiance, but as he lowered himself to sit, Ehnita realized he meant it more as an invitation rather than a direct order.

On the floor of the teepee, Ehnita glanced from one face to the other and tried to discern from facial movements what was happening in the conversation that was being had in front of her, in the language she used to hear her mother speak but she, herself, refused to learn.

"He wants to know the same as I do. Why are you here?"

Ehnita scowled at Oteitani. "It's not like I want to be here. I asked you several times to help me so that I could go back home."

"Where do you come from?"

"I told you, I took the path behind the sheriff's office."

"What is this *sheriff's office* you speak of?"

"The office on the other side of the bridge."

"What bridge?"

"What do you mean, *what bridge*? The one right before you get to the top of the waterfall."

"There is no bridge there. The water is our bridge."

It was like being stuck in the Twilight Zone. Nothing made sense. Everything was slightly off.

"Where are you from? Who are your people?"

Instantly Ehnita's mouth began to fill with saliva, and she balled her hands into a fist as she tried to silently will away the nausea. One of the questions on its own was enough to make her feel as if there was a vise grip on her heart, but the two together were almost more than she could handle. Those questions had haunted her the majority of her life; worse than being asked the questions was knowing deep down inside that she didn't have any answers. She didn't know.

"My name is, An—Ehnita. I used to live here with my mother when I was younger. Maybe you knew her. Oneida?"

Her mother's name had sparked more interest than she bargained for and caused more commotion than she expected. Oteitani and the other man went back and forth for several minutes, each taking turns glancing at her but not saying anything to her.

"Hello?" Ehnita waved her hand slowly between the two men. "Sorry to interrupt, but does all this talking mean he knew my mother?"

"Yes. Tatanka says he met a woman a very long time ago with your mother's name and a face like yours. Where is your mother now?"

"She's dead. She died a while ago. The funeral was here; I'm surprised you guys didn't hear about it. According to Wes, everybody here knew her and loved her and showed up to bury her in some ceremony. I guess he was wrong."

Oteitani looked back at Tatanka and nodded. "We can go now."

"Go where?"

Before Oteitani could reach the entrance of the teepee, Tatanka spoke to him in a low, slow way that seemed very ominous to Ehnita.

More concerned now with what she decided was surely a warning, Ehnita looked up at Oteitani, and her eyes begged for information. "What did he say?"

"He said I must watch after you."

"And what else?"

"And tonight, we will celebrate your mother passing over."

"And what else?"

"And he said that he's been waiting for you."

"Waiting for me?"

"Yes."

"Why?"

"Because he knew you would come."

"And how did he know that?"

"Because you are your mother's daughter."

Speechless, Ehnita watched the flap of the teepee close as Oteitani exited. When she went to follow behind him, she paused and took a glance behind her at Tatanka. Billows of smoke clouded his face and the air around him, and somewhere in the haziness of it all, Ehnita could have sworn she could hear Black Raven laughing. Swearing she was catching a contact high from all the smoke, Ehnita quickly shook her head and ducked out of the teepee.

Back in front of the fire, Oteitani sat on a bench that looked like it was made out of two tree stumps. Ehnita waited for him to instruct her to *sit,* but such a command never came, and with her patience now in short supply, she decided not to stand there like an idiot waiting for a command. Invitation or no, she plopped down next to him.

"I'm not sure what my mother has to do with anything, but if you could help me get back to the other side of the water, I promise, I'll be out of your hair, and I won't come back."

"So, you came from the other side of the water? How did you get here? Why did you come?" Oteitani poked at the fire with a long, ash-covered stick. "Are there others with you?"

"I told you, I was with Black Raven. We came across the bridge behind the sheriff's office, and I came because he wanted to show me something. What, I'm not sure. Anyway, one minute he was right behind me, and the next he was gone."

"Tatanka thinks you come from the sky…like your mother."

"From the sky? Like my mother? I don't understand."

"Do you know what I think?"

"No, I don't. What do you think?"

"I think you come from the north. I think your people have turned their backs on you, and you cannot go home now, so you come here."

Ehnita searched the flames for understanding but could find none. Exhaustion crept out of an exhale she didn't realize she had been holding in. "I don't know what you're talking about. I want to go home."

"Come." As he lifted his leg over the bench, Oteitani glanced down sideways at Ehnita. "Tatanka says I must stay with you. Tonight, you will sleep here, and when the sun rises, I will take you back across the river."

Not what she wanted, but being in no position to protest, Ehnita followed Oteitani to a small teepee a few yards away from where they previously sat. This teepee was unlike the first. The floor was mostly dirt. There was one large animal hide that partially covered the ground, but it was nowhere near as nice as what Tatanka had. The pallet she assumed she'd be sleeping on was thin and appeared grungy.

"I can't sleep here."

"Why not?"

"It's filthy and I don't even know whose things these are. Is this the best guest teepee you have? It's just—I can't sleep here."

A sudden flicker of frustration covered the otherwise stoic face of Oteitani. "This is my home. I share it with you. You will sleep here, and when the sun rises, I will take you back across the river so you can go back to your home."

The flap to the teepee closed before Ehnita could respond, but it didn't matter because she found herself with nothing to say anyway. Alone in the teepee she slowly crept down to the animal hide on the ground. It smelled of sweat, evergreen, musk, and vanilla.

Either she was more tired than she thought she was, or she inhaled too much smoke, but after what seemed like a blink of an eye, night had suddenly turned into day. Lying on her back she looked up at the top of the teepee where the frame came together and rolled her eyes.

"Why, God? Why?"

"Ehnita?"

Ehnita chuckled to herself as she shook her head and rolled her eyes. Clearly it wasn't God. Oteitani's thick, deep voice blew through the teepee's entrance like a warm gust of air.

"Yes? I'm awake. I'm up."

Opening the flap but not stepping inside, Oteitani looked over at Ehnita and nodded. "Hello."

"Good morning."

"Yes, it is. Come, there's some food for you by the fire. Then we can go."

Normally Ehnita was the first one up, no matter who she was with. She prided herself on being an early riser and took the *early bird gets the worm* saying very seriously. But here, she found herself a little bit behind everyone else. Outside of Oteitani's teepee, life was going on. Everyone seemed to have been awake for a while, even the children.

Back at the bench in front of the smoldering wood that had been a roaring fire just a few hours ago, Ehnita stared at what she thought looked like a very expensive charcuterie board. Only there was no cheese to speak of, or baked crackers, or anything else she was used to seeing. There was, however, fish and some assorted berries and much to her dismay, there was also fry bread.

Ehnita sniffed at the old copper cup Oteitani handed her. She thought she recognized the odor, but she couldn't quite place the scent. "What's this?"

"Drink. It's good."

Hesitant but also a little dehydrated, she inhaled deeply before tilting the cup back toward her mouth.

"Mmm, that is good." The mint inside surprised her and brought a smile to her face. It was bold and refreshing and somewhat calming. The water tasted crisp, and there was something about the mint she recognized, but it had a brilliance to it like she had never experienced before. The taste was more potent, and the smell was more radiant. It didn't just taste good; it made her feel good.

"Here, eat." With board in hand, Oteitani offered Ehnita some fish and fry bread.

"Oh no, thank you. I'm not that hungry. Never really been a breakfast person."

Shaking his head Oteitani placed the board down on the bench. "We will go now then."

As they left, the women in the village shouted at Oteitani from the entrances of their teepees, and children ran behind them and tried to tag along. In a language that was becoming more painful to her ears the more she heard it, Ehnita grabbed at her chest and tried to snatch away the ache that was beginning to beat inside her chest. She silently watched as Oteitani knelt down and spoke to the children softly and touched the tops of their heads.

"Are we all set to go now?" Ehnita's impatience showed through in her tone, but in case it wasn't completely clear, she folded her arms and began tapping her foot as she looked down at him saying his goodbyes.

"Yes, I am ready."

The first fifteen minutes of walking through the woods was spent in almost complete silence, except for Ehnita's stumbling and utterances of pain as she either stepped wrong or walked into something sharp. It was enough to frighten away any and all sleeping animals in the vicinity.

"So much noise."

"Excuse me?" Doing her best to stumble closer without falling, Ehnita grabbed at the air in front of her in an effort to regain her balance.

"You. You make so much noise."

"Well, excuse me, but I don't spend my days hiking around through the woods. I'm more of a concrete and pavement kind of woman."

"I don't know what you are saying or what it has to do with you making so much noise."

"It means—you know what? Never mind. It doesn't even matter anyway. But while I'm being noisy, can I ask why it's taking so long to get back to the waterfall? Also, I don't remember walking this way last night. I don't remember all this…this—nature."

"We are not going to the waterfall. The *kanawa* is further downstream."

"Kanawa?"

"Yes, kanawa. It is how we will cross to the other side of the river."

"Oh, you mean canoe. What about the bridge? Why are we going by can—I mean kanawa? Why can't we take the bridge?"

"As I told you before, there is no such bridge to the other side. Not unless you and whoever you are traveling with made one."

Determined not to argue about the existence of a bridge she knew was there because she'd crossed it already, Ehnita did her best to make less *noise*. They seemed to get along better when they weren't speaking to one another.

After another twenty minutes of heavy silence, they finally reached the opening of the river.

"You want me to get in that?"

Patience was considered to be an honorable and well-sought-after quality, Oteitani seemed to be trying very hard not to lose his. "You want to go to the other side of the river, don't you? If not in the kanawa, how else do you expect to go? You do not seem one to want to swim."

"The br—"

"Do not say it. There is no bridge. It is either the kanawa or swim. Or you can walk further downstream to where the water is shallow, and then we can walk across there, but that would take half the day."

While none of the options pleased her, Ehnita conceded. "Fine, it's just this thing literally looks like you chopped it down last week and hollowed it out."

"Sit."

"Why do I have to get in first?"

"Okay, I will get in first and you can push it into the water and then jump in."

"Oh." Ehnita cautiously climbed in and quickly searched the space in front of her for something to hold onto in case things went bad. "You know, you could have explained that you had to push it in; you didn't have to be so rude about it."

Finally, in the water, Ehnita sat up front, tense and anxious to get to the other side. She hadn't realized how wide the river actually was until then.

"We're almost to the other side. How far upstream is this cabin?"

"Uh, it shouldn't be more than ten, fifteen minutes. Once we get back on land, I'll be fine. I can make it the rest of the way on my own."

Oteitani neither agreed nor disagreed; he simply kept rowing until they made their way ashore.

"Okay, well, we're here." Unsure of whether to shake his hand or not, Ehnita nervously patted the side of her thigh instead. "Thank you again for bringing me back. I really appreciate it."

Standing there alongside the kanawa, Oteitani nodded toward Ehnita, his eyes catching her gaze as he did so. "You are welcome."

"Okay, I guess this is where I leave you then. I'm gonna head out now. Maybe stop and say goodbye to Black Raven before I head home. It was nice meeting you, Oteitani."

In truth, Ehnita didn't know how long it would take her to get back to Black Raven's cabin. The time she gave Oteitani was a rough estimate, but she was confident she could get there on her own. His cabin, after all, was at the base of the waterfall; it would be hard to miss. All she had to do was follow the river upstream. The decision to do it on her own came naturally to her. She was always on her own. The thought of relying on someone else made her feel more uneasy than riding in the canoe.

In spite of herself Ehnita made it to the base of the waterfall in twenty minutes. Running on pure adrenaline, she surprised herself with how quickly she covered so much ground. Unfortunately, her newfound ability to hike quickly was not the only surprise that lay in store for her that morning. There, at the base of the waterfall, standing in the mist from the rushing water, Ehnita circled and searched, panicked and confused, but she found nothing: no cabin, no trail, no Black Raven, nothing.

For over an hour Ehnita walked around in circles, going back and forth between the waterfall and the spot where Black Raven's cabin should have been but wasn't; eventually she made her way to the trail that no longer seemed to exist, and therefore, it led nowhere.

Defeated and on the verge of hysterics, she sat down along the side of the water and stared at the thundering falls as she pulled her knees close to her chest and rocked back and forth.

"Maybe Tatanka knows another way to find your Black Raven."

Coming from behind her, more calming to her now than he had been before, Oteitani squatted down alongside Ehnita. "Are you ready to go back now?"

Chapter Fourteen

Still stunned and confused by the morning's events, Ehnita sat motionless and silent on the floor of Oteitani's teepee.

"You should eat something." Unsure of what to bring that she would actually eat, Oteitani brought as much food as he could find…berries, jerky, fry bread, and beans.

Ehnita looked at the food, her eyes burning and red from the tears being held at the brim.

"I don't understand."

"Eat something. You will feel better and be able to think clearer once you have some food."

"What happened to the cabin? To Black Raven?"

Her desperation hung in the air of the teepee like a smoke cloud. Bringing himself down to his knees, not convinced but hopeful that food would help, he extended a piece of fry bread toward her.

"I have never seen this cabin that you speak of, but I have heard of Black Raven."

Tears began to fall as she absentmindedly chewed the bread. "And that's why you waited even though I told you to go? You knew there was no cabin? You knew there was nothing there?"

"I did not know."

"Then why did you wait? Why didn't you leave?"

"I would never leave you. What kind of man would I be if I did that? I wanted to make sure you made it home safely. I watched you for a long time go around and around, never finding what you were looking for, surprised again and again each time when it was not there."

"But it was there. The cabin, the trail, it was there yesterday." Ehnita looked at Oteitani, tears streaming down her face. "I feel like I'm losing my mind."

"Tatanka may have more answers for you than I do. We will go and sit with him."

Outside of the teepee on their way back to the fire, Ehnita looked at the men and women who were standing around staring at her as she walked past, and she resented the look in their eyes; she didn't need a translator to understand what it was they were thinking…they pitied her. She knew the look well; she had seen it many times before.

"Does anyone here go to work? Does no one have anything better to do than to stand around and stare at me?"

"They are working right now."

"You could have fooled me."

Not understanding her meaning or her mood, Oteitani disregarded her comment. "Sit here. I will bring Tatanka."

As she watched Oteitani walk away from her and found herself surrounded by strangers, Ehnita felt the pains of the past prick at her skin. How did she get back here? How did she get to this place where she was an outcast amongst what she considered to be a group of outsiders. While she sat in front of the smoldering wood and waited for Oteitani to return with Tatanka, she began to grow obstinate and resentful with each passing minute.

"Moon."

Ehnita turned to see Tatanka approaching with Oteitani.

"Yeah."

"*Moon.* Tatanka says this is the name Black Raven spoke many years ago. Tatanka says he'd forgotten how to say it; I was teaching him just now."

While they waited for Tatanka to settle in, Oteitani knelt by the open firepit and poked at the smoldering wood until it flickered. Humming to himself as he arranged more wood around the broken logs, he prodded until the flames caught and the fire began to blaze and crackle in front of them.

Ehnita found she was unable to contain herself any longer. "Why was he talking to Black Raven about me?"

Listening intently yet understanding nothing, Ehnita's eyes bounced back and forth between Tatanka and Oteitani. And for the first time in her life, she regretted not spending more time with her mother and learning from her. "What's he saying? What's he talking about?"

Ehnita's ill manners and abrasive demeanor seemed to rub Oteitani the wrong way. He didn't understand her ways. With a sigh, he raised his hand toward Tatanka, halting him from continuing, and then he turned and looked at Ehnita with an exhaustion in his eyes that he made no effort to hide.

"He was not finished, but he says many years ago when Black Raven still lived amongst us, his son fell in love with your mother. They had a child together, here; you were born here. But soon after you were born, your father died."

"My father's dead?"

"Yes. You didn't know?"

"Well, yes, but no, I mean—yes, my mother told me my father died."

"And you did not believe her?"

"Yes…sort of. My mother and I had a very different kind of relationship."

He hadn't understood what she meant, but he didn't like the feeling her statement left with him. He frowned in confusion, but quickly shook it off.

"Tatanka says your mother was so sad after your father died, she decided to return home and to take you with her."

"Okay, and how does Black Raven fit into this?"

"As I said, Ehnita, he was not finished speaking."

Oteitani had been tactful yet pleasant in the way he conversed with her. He had conceded to her petulance and somehow without any effort had made her feel embarrassed by her own actions. She would be quiet from now on while Tatanka spoke; she would listen, and she would be patient.

As late afternoon turned into early evening, Oteitani, Ehnita, and Tatanka found themselves in the company of almost everyone in the tribe. Everyone had quietly made their way to the fire and taken seats on the ground to listen to Tatanka speak. In between the spaces where Tatanka rested, either for breath, food, or refreshment, Oteitani would translate for Ehnita.

"Black Raven is from here, like you, but he left a long time ago, and since then he has returned and gone one time. Your mother has come and gone one time also; both left many, many moons ago and have not returned…both were waiting for you. Now you are here, and they are not."

There was a certain sadness in the eyes of those who sat surrounding her by the fire. A sadness she couldn't understand but she could feel.

"So, it's my fault they never came back?"

"That is not what he is saying. It is not your fault they are not here, but it is because of you that they never returned."

"Well, doesn't that mean the same thing?"

"No."

Before she could continue her debate on sameness, Tatanka began speaking again, and the sadness she previously saw in each eye was now replaced with an intense sort of horror. As the fire crackled and Tatanka spoke, with each word Ehnita could see mothers pull their children closer to them. Men who were sitting stood up and squared their chests; the only man who was still kneeling—but with each inch of his body tensed as if he were about to pounce—was Oteitani. In a brief moment of silence, he looked at Ehnita curiously, and as the fire grew and crackled, a flash of rage reflected in Oteitani's eyes.

"Where you live, we do not exist. We have been scattered across the earth. We are lost to ourselves, hiding our nature, bargaining to live on land that we have cared for, protected, and blessed. Your waters run dry, and your trees have been cut short. You take from the earth and return nothing to it."

"That's not true." Feeling very much judged and attacked, Ehnita looked out amongst the faces she knew did not understand her and searched for one face that appeared less ill at ease with her presence…she didn't find one. "That's not fair. Yes, we do cut down trees and change the landscape a little, but what we leave in its place is so much better. We build places that give people jobs to help them earn income to support their families and build better lives. We try to build in a way that takes advantage of nature and offers something beautiful to look at, at the same time."

"Why would you want to take advantage of nature?"

"I didn't mean it that way."

"Then how did you mean it?"

All eyes were on Ehnita. They may not have understood her words, but they understood the tone in Oteitani's response. It was in that moment that she realized they weren't talking about the same thing. He was speaking to something more—something much, much more.

She couldn't answer his question. She thought about it and realized there was no good answer. Somewhat embarrassed but eager for more information, Ehnita took a breath and looked at Tatanka. "Why did they stay for me?"

Clearly a question he had himself, Oteitani wasted no time translating to Tatanka. As he spoke, the eyes of those who listened began to soften some. The men who stood began to ease their shoulders. Oteitani dropped his head and searched the ground in confusion before turning back to look at Ehnita.

"They stayed to save you, so that you could save them all."

Before Ehnita could respond, Oteitani was once again focused on Tatanka, who had resumed speaking. Heads began to nod in agreement, and a hum began to generate from the mouths of the previously quiet crowd.

"He says in his life, he has not seen many who can travel through worlds. The ones he has met who can do it are often tormented by things they see and cannot change. They become trapped between two worlds but belong to neither. He wishes this gift to no one. When heaven and earth trade places, it is hard to know where to find peace; is it in the sky above or the ground below?"

"So, how am I meant to save everyone?"

She threw her hands up in frustration and looked over to Oteitani for answers. "What he's basically telling me is, I've inherited a curse?"

"No, Ehnita. What he says is, you inherit the sky. You inherit everything."

Chapter Fifteen

Monday morning, three days since the last time he'd seen Ehnita, Wes made his way down to Black Raven's cabin to check in with him. Once he hit the landing at the bottom of the trail, from a few feet away, he could see Black Raven sitting on his front porch in his rocking chair, staring out across the water, humming low to himself. Wes smiled and waved as he approached.

"Good morning."

Black Raven nodded in agreement as he smiled to himself and continued to hum. "Yes, good morning."

As Wes sat in the chair next to Raven, he handed him a plate covered in tin foil. "From Auntie Layla. She says you need to eat more."

"She worries too much."

Wes nodded in agreement, smiled, and settled into his seat.

"You truly have the best view on the reservation. Just quiet here. So much peace. Has Ehnita gotten used to it?"

"I do not know."

Surprised and concerned by his statement, Wes leaned forward and looked at Black Raven curiously. "Where is she, Black Raven? I know she hasn't gone back home; her car is still sitting in front of my office. Should I be worried?"

"You spend too much time with Layla." Black Raven chuckled and leaned forward to grab his pipe off the small table by his side. "You do not need to worry about Moon. She is fine."

"Where is she?"

"She is here."

Quickly turning around toward the door to look inside the cabin, Wes glanced at the spaces he could see from where he sat.

"Not inside the house." After stuffing his pipe, Black Raven slowly reached for the box of matches.

"Where is she then?"

With the flame from the match illuminating his face, Black Raven turned and looked at Wes carefully before touching the flame to his pipe. After taking in several short bursts to get the smoke going, Black Raven smiled widely with satisfaction and slowly leaned back in his rocker.

"I will tell you where she is. It is a long story, but if you wish to know, I will tell you."

Wes quickly got up from his seat and went to the table where he had placed the plate of food from Layla. "It is a good thing I brought this from Auntie's then."

After he was seated and had a few bites of the grilled meat, Wes looked at Black Raven, who was once again smiling and humming to himself as he looked across the water. His eyes were seeing something Wes's could not, and Black Raven could sense his anticipation. Nodding, he slowly shut his eyes and chuckled to himself. Black Raven stopped rocking and exhaled as he readied himself and began to explain the unexplainable.

"Now, I will tell you where Moon is, but first I must try to show you what you do not see. This is the only way you can find her."

"Would you slow down, please?"

Unsure what to do with herself that morning, Ehnita did the only thing she could think of, which was to follow the only person who could understand her.

Oteitani was less than thrilled to have Ehnita at his side, but he didn't protest or complain. "It is a good thing we are not hunting. All would go hungry today if we were."

Unbothered by his comment, Ehnita picked up the pace. "So, you expect me to believe that I somehow managed to travel back in time?"

"We do not expect anything from you."

Not quite sure if he was insulting her or not, Ehnita quickly shook off the uncertainty.

"According to you and Tatanka, my mother, Black Raven, and I possess some mystical ability to travel back in time to—to…I don't know when; I guess a time before America was discovered, maybe?"

Disinterested but listening respectfully, Oteitani shrugged. "I have not heard of this place."

"*This place.*" Ehnita laughed. "America is *this place* where we are right now. It's the land that you stand on."

"The Cheveopai stand on no one's land but their own."

Realizing too late that her laughter and mimicking were in fact offensive, Ehnita offered him the only thing she could to make amends…her silence.

They walked for miles in the lushness of the forest. They passed tree after tree, each one looking the same, but something about each one being a little different than the one before it, after it, and beside it. One was higher than the one before. One was more aged. One had more width. On her own, Ehnita would have been lost. She would have been caught up and lost in all the sameness.

After almost an hour of walking in silence, they'd reached their destination, which to Ehnita looked like nowhere at all. Right there in the middle of the forest was a large, open field filled with tiny flowers of lilac, yellow, and white, all of which stood out sharply but blended together perfectly with the rich green grass. It didn't take her long to notice patches of deep purple calla lilies scattered across the field, the same flower that she had seen pressed between wax paper and tucked into a box, the same box that held her mother's most precious things.

The thought that her mother had been here, in the same place that she was standing now, sent a shiver down Ehnita's spine. She could see why her mother saved the flowers. The field was gorgeous and worth remembering, and if she were her mother, she'd try to hold on to the image too; preserve it for as long as she could.

"I didn't mean to laugh at you. I wasn't trying to offend you. I didn't think you were being serious."

Enough time had passed that Oteitani's furrowed brow and clenched jaw had relaxed. "You should have brought a basket."

"A basket for what?"

"For the plants we are bringing back."

"Oh. But I didn't know we were coming to collect flowers."

"You did not ask."

"True. I didn't. Why are we collecting flowers all the way out here? Surely there's some closer to camp."

Kneeling in the tall grass, studying the tops of the flowers in front of him, Oteitani bent to smell the lilac flower before nodding in affirmation. "These plants heal, Ehnita. Our supply is low, so we will bring back more."

Unsure how to help and not wanting to cause more trouble, Ehnita sat off to the side and watched as Oteitani carefully wrapped the flowers he'd cut into a piece of cloth.

"Ow." Her gladiator sandals seemed like a smart choice when she put them on three days ago, but now she was regretting the decision.

Sitting down across from her, Oteitani took her right foot into his hand and studied the sandal.

"No wonder you walk so slow. These are no good for your feet. Look, your feet are red and filled with pain."

Without asking, Oteitani cut the straps of Ehnita's sandals.

"Wait, I don't have anything else to wear."

"It is better to have nothing than to walk in these."

After the other sandal had been cut off, Ehnita couldn't deny that her feet felt much better. "Thank you."

"You are welcome."

With both of her feet now firmly in his hands, Oteitani studied the red, swollen spots and gently went over them with his finger and examined the damage.

"Oteitani?"

"Yes, Ehnita?"

"What did Tatanka mean when he said I could travel through worlds? Was he talking about me being an outsider because I don't live on the reservation?"

"No."

"Well then, what did he mean? Clearly, I haven't traveled back in time. I mean, you're here with me speaking English. You've gone to school; you've been educated. I've seen things here that wouldn't be here if we were in the fifteenth century."

"I do not understand all that Tatanka has said. He has seen more than me. But I agree with him that you are not from our world. I have been north before many times to the place the people from across the ocean have settled. Every tribe has sent members to watch, some to learn, and others have been sent as punishment. They call it Jamestown. This is where I learn to speak your language."

"Jamestown? Seriously? All the whites in America—or whatever you call this place—they live in Jamestown?"

Oteitani nodded as he searched around the open field.

"That's not possible. What about the rest of the country?"

"When they first came across the ocean and news of their arrival began to spread from tribe to tribe, many went north to see for themselves. We do not know why they came here. We let them stay, but it was agreed amongst most all of the tribes that they must stay in Jamestown lands. Some have tried to leave, but they did not make it far, and if they made it too far, they never made it back, and so the others learned not to try."

Ehnita's mind raced. Oteitani got up and began to move around the field in search of something.

"So, you're telling me that the pilgrims did arrive, but America never happened? Lewis and Clark never happened? The Indian Removal Act, the Trail of Tears, Santa Ana, Sitting Bull, they never happened? These events never happened? These people—time went on and nothing changed? No industry? No technology? Nothing changed?"

Returning to his previous place across from her with several large, waxy green leaves in his hand, Oteitani shook his head. "I do not know of these things you speak of. I know of Santa Ana; he was a good man, fearless warrior. His people and their territory are not too far from here. And Sitting Bull, I know of him as well; I have met some of his grandchildren on my way north. They don't trust those who have settled in Jamestown. It is mostly they who guard that area."

Ehnita sat stunned as Oteitani went to work trying to piece together something for her feet. She was unsure of what she found more shocking: what Oteitani had said or the fact that she believed him. Both ideas left Ehnita speechless.

"We have learned a great deal from those who have settled up north. We have learned their language, some of their customs and their faith. Some of what we have learned has been good, and some has been not so good. Even from the not so good, we have learned."

"What did you learn?"

"I learned that a person with nothing can still give you everything. They can give you all of themselves, every single part of them. I also learned that a person with everything, who offers nothing, is worthless to you. I learned that I love my people and my land more than I even knew myself."

The idea that history had never happened blew Ehnita's mind. In this place where your word was everything, Ehnita could see why the West was never won. The Indigenous tribes had learned from the white settlers, but with no one willing to teach them in return, progress had never arrived here…wherever *here* was.

"And you're happy here like this?"

Oteitani looked at Ehnita carefully. The confusion in her eyes and the tenseness of her limbs were evident. "Yes, I am happy here. I have no greater joy, no greater peace than when I am here, when I am home. This is my home. This is where I belong."

With the waxy leaves acting as soles and some torn cloth that once held the plants that Oteitani had set aside an entire morning to come to the field to collect, Ehnita had something on her feet to act as shoes in lieu of walking barefoot.

"There. These will help your feet until we get back home. And I will walk slowly with you all the way."

"So Ehnita is here?"

Slowly nodding as he rocked and sucked his pipe, Black Raven told Wes, "Yes, she is here."

"And will she come back?"

"Only she knows the answer to that."

Wes sat back and looked across the water, trying to catch a glimpse of what wasn't there. "I wish I could be there too."

Black Raven nodded and began humming again, his eyes cast across the water toward his home.

Chapter Sixteen

After having spent the past two days hiding out in Oteitani's teepee, going back and forth with herself about the reality of her situation, Ehnita had finally concluded that Oteitani was telling the truth. Impossible as she thought the situation to be, she knew it was the truth.

The night before had been the hardest night Ehnita had experienced there so far. As she slept, feelings and images of herself falling into darkness consumed her and violently woke her from her sleep. She'd woken up several times in hysterics, sweating and screaming, but the second she opened her eyes, Oteitani was there with knife in hand and ready to slay all the figments of her imagination. When the morning had finally arrived, she woke up that Thursday morning to find Oteitani sitting outside the teepee. His knife was still firmly in his hand as he rested. His face looked serene and his eyes were shut, but his body was still tense and on high alert, ready to spring into action for her…all for her.

Sitting up all night couldn't have been comfortable, yet when she looked down at him, he didn't look tired or unhappy. When he looked up at her, he appeared genuinely concerned, which was not at all what Ehnita would have expected. She'd kept him up for more than half the night fighting invisible monsters. She would have understood if he were annoyed or angry, but he wasn't. She could see a sadness inside of him…he hurt for her. It was in that moment when he borrowed her pain that Ehnita felt like she could breathe again. He had calmed her troubled mind.

As Oteitani got to his feet, he gently nodded to Ehnita. "Good morning."

From outside the teepee, through the flap Ehnita held open, Oteitani stared at her and shook his head.

"You will make yourself sick if you continue to stay here like this. Come with me."

With no defensible reason not to go, Ehnita put on the suede moccasins that had been made for her by Tatanka's wife; it was she who came and tended to her injured feet and soothed them back to health. She loved the moccasins and smiled to herself each time she put them on.

Despite the language barrier, Ehnita enjoyed her time with Tatanka's wife. The song she softly sang as she lovingly rubbed oils over Ehnita's blistered soles made her think of her mother and how Oneida's fingers would massage her scalp before she brushed her hair. It was in those moments when her feet were being rubbed that she felt completely at home.

"Where are we going?"

"Come."

The destination was of no consequence to her, and in retrospect, she wasn't sure why she had even bothered to ask.

"Oteitani, I was wondering if you could ask Tatanka if he knows how Black Raven and my mother got back over to the other side?"

"How did you get here?"

"I don't know."

"I will ask him."

In very little time they arrived at the base of the waterfall. Some of the children from the tribe were already there splashing around in the water.

"Why are we here?"

"For you."

"You want me to go swimming? I don't see how that's going to help anything."

Sensing her resistance and not wanting to argue, Oteitani picked Ehnita up and threw her over his shoulder and walked directly under the rushing waterfall.

"What are you doing? Put me down!"

She was completely drenched and spitting out water as she tried to breathe and scream at the same time. When they finally reached the place where the water seemed to come down the hardest, Oteitani gently put Ehnita down. Once again on her feet, she couldn't decide if she should run or hide, so she stood there and let the water pour down on her because she was too afraid to move.

The sound of Oteitani laughing pierced through Ehnita's shock. "Why are you laughing? Stop laughing."

But he didn't stop laughing. Her shouting at him only made him laugh harder, and despite herself she smiled. For the first time in a long time, she sincerely smiled. Standing there under the pressure of the water, she felt completely free. She had never felt more alive in her life than she did in that moment.

"Moon, you are better now. You look much better now."

Ehnita stood there with her face turned up toward the sky and her arms spread wide open and thrust behind her back for almost an hour. It didn't seem like an hour to her and the peace she seemed to find in that time brought Oteitani so much joy, from the look on his face anyone who was looking could clearly see that his prayers were being answered that day.

Oteitani was reluctant to disturb the moment he had prayed she would find, but he knew there was more in store for her that day. As he inhaled deeply, he took one last long look at her smiling face and said a silent *thank you* to the sky.

"Ehnita, we should go now. The others will be waiting."

The bass in Oteitani's voice coaxed Ehnita's eyes open, and there was a newness to them that she could feel. She could see him in front of her but in a way she hadn't seen before; he was extraordinary.

"Is something happening today?"

"Yes. We will be celebrating."

"Celebrating what?"

"Celebrating you."

Shivering but feeling invigorated, Ehnita stood in front of Oteitani, rubbing her arms, trying to get herself warm. She stared at him, confused.

"A celebration for me? Why? It's not my birthday or anything."

"Because you are here."

"Okay. And?"

"And today we celebrate your arrival."

"But why today? I've been here almost a week now."

"Yes, you have been here, but you were leaving ever since you arrived…passing through. Now you are here, and we do not know for how long, so today we celebrate. We celebrate because today you are here; tomorrow you may not be, but today you are."

As he walked over to a nearby tree, Ehnita bounced behind him, still shivering but on a natural high like she'd never been on before in her life. "Thank you for bringing me here. I needed that. The water felt amazing. It almost felt like I was flying."

Oteitani smiled as he handed her the dark brown suede dress that had been resting at the base of the tree next to them.

"This is for you, made by Tatanka's wife. You can change over there; the bushes are thick. I will wait for you here."

With dress in hand, she went off in the direction Oteitani had pointed to. As she walked and looked around at her surroundings, she realized that the path she currently was on was the same path she had been on two days prior with Black Raven. The path was the same, yet it was different. The bushes weren't as lush and thick as they were right now, and the trees hadn't been nearly as abundant. There was much more life here today than five days ago.

"What did you feel when you were standing under the water?"

"Joy." The word fell from Ehnita's mouth before she had time to process the question. Nevertheless, it was the truth.

Oteitani nodded, as if he understood her explanation completely even though she herself did not. "You are not like anyone I have ever met."

"Is that a good thing or a bad thing?"

"It is neither."

She decided to take his indifference as a win, and the victory made her smile. Generally, his opinion would not be one that she would have sought out or valued or even taken seriously, not in her world; but here in his, it meant a great deal.

"So, this party that I'm not dressed for...who's going to be there?"

"Everyone." Oteitani paused and looked down at Ehnita quizzically as she stepped out from behind the bushes. "You have a dress. You have it on now."

Trying her hardest not to laugh, Ehnita smiled and shook her head. "No, I didn't mean *a dress*. I mean dressed up, you know, with some nice high heels. Something a little more form fitting, some product for my hair and some makeup. That's how I would normally attend a celebration."

"With hair product and makeup? Why? Why do you need this? What does it mean?"

"It means—" She'd never truly considered the meaning behind her actions before. "I guess it means that... You know what? I'm honestly not sure what it means, but it's to make you look beautiful. It gives you confidence when you know that you look good."

"Makeup does this?"

"Yeah. Sort of. Why do you guys wear makeup? I've seen some old photos of people on the reservation with their faces painted, and when I was younger my mom used to take me to these large festivals where everyone would be all dressed up in bright colors, and all the men and women would have makeup on their faces. Some would have three black lines painted on their chin, some had bright red going across the entire top half of their face, and some had symbols on their chest. But most, if not all, had *something*."

"Yes, yes. We wear this *makeup*. We paint our faces too but not to make ourselves feel beautiful. We paint for mourning, or war, to celebrate, or hunting, or when it is time for you to become a man. But never to make oneself beautiful. Only being who you are can do that."

Ehnita looked down at herself in the homemade dress and once again thought of her mother. She remembered the skirt in the box that had belonged to her mother, and all of a sudden it was like she could see her; she could see her mother with her animal skin skirt, smiling and holding a calla lily out toward her, wanting her to reach for it. Ehnita smiled as she wrapped her arms around herself and stared down at her new dress and gazed into the image of her mother's smile.

By the time they arrived back to the community, everyone was already around the fire. Some of the women were dancing, children ran back and forth chasing one another, and the smell of tobacco filled the air and mingled with the scent of smoked meat.

Once they had gotten close, Ehnita stopped dead in her tracks and looked at everyone in awe. Never before had she felt more humbled…they were all gathered there just for her. Of all the things that had happened over the past few days, so far this was the most unbelievable…a celebration just because she was there. She hadn't had to prove anything; she hadn't sold anything, signed, negotiated, or done anything. She was just there.

Oteitani looked back and smiled at her, as if he knew. "Yes, Moon, for you. To welcome you home."

Chapter Seventeen

"Is this where you've been sleeping at night?"

Ehnita stood in the tree line surrounding the village, confused and somewhat embarrassed. After having searched for him since the moment she woke up, Ehnita had finally found Oteitani. She didn't realize until that moment that she hadn't given any thought to where he went when they weren't together. Until today, he had always been the one to wake her and lead her somewhere, but today Ehnita was up with the dawn and the other women in the village.

"Yes, this is where I sleep."

"Why?"

"Because I have given you my home."

Her cheeks quickly flushed deep red with embarrassment. "Oh my God, I'm so sorry. I didn't even realize what my sleeping in your teepee meant for you. I thought you just went to an empty one or were like staying with a friend. I didn't know you were out here with nothing, sleeping under a tree."

"Here I have everything, Ehnita." Smiling as he lifted his face toward the sky, Oteitani shut his eyes and inhaled the air around him. "What do I have in there that I do not have here?"

With her lips pursed, she thought about it for a minute and quickly decided he might be right. Excited to get down to the reason why she was there, she plopped down next to him on the ground.

"So, I was hoping, if you weren't too busy this morning, you might be able to help me with something?"

"Never too busy to help."

The sincerity of his response made her flinch slightly. There was no ego involved. He truly wanted to help with whatever she needed, which was a concept more foreign to her than the place she was in.

"Good. Glad to hear that, because I'd like to thank everyone for being so kind to me while I've been here. Everyone's been very good to me. They've given me clothes and food and shelter, and they didn't have to. I just want to find some way to say thanks."

Confused by her statement but still listening, Oteitani studied Ehnita's face. He focused on her eyes and searched, trying to find meaning and understanding in the words she spoke.

Since the celebration for her four days ago. Ehnita had concluded that she was there for a reason, that Black Raven wanted her to see something, and she wouldn't be able to leave until she had. It was at the celebration she finally understood what he had been saying. Typically, when she looked at members of the tribe, her own mother included, she saw stereotypes and labels—alcoholics, charity cases, ragamuffins…savages. She saw everything she never wanted anyone to associate her with. But when she finally stopped seeing the stigmas in her head and opened her eyes and saw the faces of the people there, the men and women dancing and singing in celebration of her arrival, it sent a sensation through her body like nothing she'd ever felt before.

Since her celebration Ehnita had been up every morning on her own. Oteitani didn't have to come and wake her and coerce her to join everyone. She didn't need his presence every second of every day; she didn't need him with her as she washed clothes with the women of the village down by the lake, or when she helped out grinding herbs by the fire; she didn't need him to translate when she would sit and braid the hair of some of the younger girls in the village or go off with them picking berries to make jam.

"I was thinking, as a thank you, I would cook dinner for everyone tonight. When I was little, I used to help my mother in the kitchen sometimes. I don't remember a lot, but I do remember this one dish she loved to make, and I'm pretty sure I can make it."

Still confused but very intrigued, Oteitani tilted his head slightly and gazed at Ehnita from the corner of his eye. "Here we work together. We are one. You do not have to repay anything. Everyone here is happy to have you working beside them."

This was a concept which was foreign to her. "I'm glad to hear that, but I still want to do it."

Smiling, he let a chuckle slip from his lips. "I must say, I think I would like to see that."

Taking his interest and amusement as a challenge, Ehnita quickly got back to her feet and brushed off the back of her dress. "Okay then, well, we should go now so that we can get started."

"And where are we going?"

"I need fish. Fresh fish."

Smiling, Oteitani nodded as he looked up at her and slowly got off the ground. "We are going fishing then?"

"Yes. We are going fishing."

She knew that morning when she decided to take the task on that fishing wouldn't be easy, which is why she decided to recruit Oteitani. But she never anticipated it would be anything like what she was stepping into.

The hike uphill before the drop to the waterfall took almost half an hour. A week ago, for Ehnita, that time would have been doubled, but now she was able to make it to the base of the falls in thirty minutes with ease. Not only could she make the journey faster now, but she could also do it on her own. As she walked up the hill, she looked out into the spray from the waterfall, and from a distance somewhere between the sunlight and the mist, she could see something. She knew it was impossible, but she could have sworn that she saw her mother looking back at her and smiling.

Once they reached the top where the water ran harder and faster, Oteitani began to unravel the net he had brought with him.

"Are you ready?"

"Am I ready for what?"

"To go in and catch the fish for your meal?"

"You want me to go in there? I'm not going in there. What if I get swept away and go over? I'll drown."

"You won't."

"You don't know that."

"I would never let you drown."

Oddly, that was enough for her. Not enough to remove her fears completely but enough to give her the courage to try. In this place where your word and your heart were all you had, she knew Oteitani meant everything he said.

"Okay, so what do we do now?"

Waist deep in the water and his back facing the drop, with net in hand and his eyes on Ehnita, once he could see that she had relaxed a bit, Oteitani looked down at the water.

"Do you see them? You stay there. I will come around and circle them in the net and bring it toward you."

Also waist deep in the water but still somewhat close to the bank, Ehnita did as she was told and watched Oteitani move forward slowly, forcing himself against the rushing current. Once he'd made his way around to Ehnita, he stuck out his hand, reaching for the other end of the net she held so that he could tie the two ends together. As she reached toward him, she lost her footing and slipped under the water. Before she had a chance to panic, she could feel Oteitani's arm around her waist lifting her back up.

"That was close. Thank you."

Although her heart was racing, and she was almost out of breath, Ehnita wasn't at all surprised that Oteitani had caught her. As she clung to his forearm, she looked down at the limp net wrapped around his other hand. "Oh no, the fish. I am so sorry."

"It's fine, we can catch more fish. The ones that got away can survive underwater, but you, Sky Woman, you cannot. I would rather catch you and let the fish go."

More determined now than she had been before and more confident as well, Ehnita looked up at Oteitani and smiled. "Okay, let's try this again."

The second attempt was much more successful than the first. They'd caught a decent number of fish and managed to get them and themselves safely back to the bank without incident.

As they began their walk back to the village, Ehnita felt proud of herself and was excited to get back.

"Tell me about your mother."

"My mother?"

"Yes."

Her mind tried to run away from the confusion closing in as she quickly searched her memories and tried to find something to say. "My mother died."

"Yes. I know that. Tell me about when she lived."

"She was—I don't know. My mother and I didn't have the best relationship. She and I were always very different. We never had anything in common."

"But you are here like she once was, and now you are making her favorite dish."

"Yeah, I guess I am. Maybe we had more in common than I knew."

Back in the village, as Oteitani cut the bellies out of the fish and cleaned them, Ehnita chopped herbs and vegetables and told him about her life before and after the reservation.

"This is why you say you do not know your mother? Because she came back to her people? She came home and you did not want to?"

"The res was never really my home. I grew up with her foster parents in a large house, with access to the best of everything. And then one day she took everything from me, out of nowhere and with no explanation. I guess for a long time I resented her, and when that was over, when I was gone and she kept begging me to come back, I couldn't understand why she would want me to come back to a place she knew I hated; I thought she was just being mean. I would always ask why, and she would never explain—or maybe I just didn't understand. I don't know. But eventually I ended up pitying her."

"You pitied her?"

"Yeah, I guess I did." Ehnita looked down somberly at the ear of corn in her hand. "She never told me about this place. She never told me about Black Raven, my father, or anything. The only thing she ever said was, *Listen to the earth, Moon.* And where I live that's crazy. People thought she was crazy; she made me think she was crazy, and I felt bad for her."

"You thought she was crazy because she wanted to share space with you? To sit in oneness with you. This is not okay in your world?"

When he said it out loud like that, it was Ehnita who sounded crazy, even to herself. As she stuffed the herbs into the gutted fish and mixed the corn and sautéed the vegetables, she did her best to explain *her world*, which meant explaining *the world*, at least the world as she knew it.

As she spoke and stirred and sautéed, more and more people gathered to listen. Oteitani translated, and the more she spoke, the more people gathered. Somewhere in the midst of her storytelling, the stirring spoon ended up in the hand of one of the older women, the fish was being turned by Tatanka's wife, and the vegetables were being turned by one of the women she did the washing with down at the lake.

Ehnita sat by the fire with all eyes on her as she told them about the *discovery* of America, about how the West was won. She gave them a brief and broad outline of Wounded Knee, Standing Rock, and the Trail of Tears. Explaining why she never told people who she really was when she met them, it embarrassed her as she said it out loud, but sitting there and watching everyone in the tribe watch her, she couldn't lie; the sincerity in their faces, the kindness they had offered her was overwhelming, and she felt compelled to tell the truth. It was the least she could do. The excuses and explanations that she gave, as inadequate as they felt in that moment, everyone seemed to understand. She explained what people thought of Indigenous people in her world and how she didn't want to be reduced to a cartoon character, a charity case, or a statistic.

"When I lived in the reservation, I always felt like an outsider, an imposter, because I hadn't been raised here, but in the city, I was a novelty, which is something I didn't want to be either. I wanted to fit somewhere, and it didn't seem like I could because of who I was and because of who I wasn't."

As it would turn out, Ehnita's mother's recipe was not her mother's recipe. Despite her absence from the preparation, the meal had turned out just the way her mother used to make it. Clearly Oneida had brought back more than Ehnita could have guessed. The fish recipe had been shared and taught to Oneida in the same way she had shared and taught Ehnita.

The food was finished, but no one was eating. Oteitani gazed at her, and a look of pure anguish washed over him. "And this is where you want to go back to? You want to return to a place where you have to hide who you are from those who have taken land they did not earn and do not deserve… You choose them over your own mother?"

And just like that, just like the fish, Oteitani had pulled Ehnita's guts right out of her belly. In that moment she felt completely empty and exposed.

"It's not that simple. My world is the only world I have ever known. It's not all that bad. I mean, at one point, things were bad if you were *Native American*. But it's better now. It's hard to explain."

"I understand."

"You do?"

"Yes. I understand. I understand why you do not know your mother; you do not know her because you do not know yourself. And maybe there, in that world, you could never know her because of how things are there, but here you are learning who she is. You made for us her favorite fish, and you smile when you tell us of her wavy hair and dimple smile. Here you are seeing your mother clearly for the first time."

"Yeah, I think I am."

After speaking to the group and a collective "Yee" and nod of the head, Oteitani turned back to Ehnita. "Tonight, we celebrate your mother."

"But I thought you all already did that?"

"Her death. We honored her memory. Tonight, because of you, Moon, we celebrate her arrival. She is here."

Chapter Eighteen

Over the next four days, Ehnita found herself smiling and humming and laughing more than she ever had in her entire life, and she spent her nights filled with excitement for the next dawn. Every member of the tribe was genuinely happy she was there, a feeling she'd been longing for, for so long that she easily got lost in the newfound affection.

As Tatanka said they would, on the third evening of her unplanned visit, the tribe gathered in honor of her mother, Oneida. Sorrow filled Ehnita's soul like breath entering the breast of a sparrow. Never had she felt such sadness in her life. Oneida had been gone well over a year, but that evening it felt like Ehnita was losing her for the first time, and she hurt in a way that she didn't know her heart could… She missed her mother. After having spent time within the community that her mother unfortunately never made it back to, Ehnita's heart began to heal.

The day after she cooked with the tribe in honor of her mother, Oteitani decided to take a walk with her around the land. What started as a slow walk, examining the sounds and the landscape surrounding them, eventually turned into Ehnita chasing him through the woods to the edge of the lake about a mile downstream from the base of the falls. She felt zero guilt as she pushed him into the water. She'd decided he deserved it after watching her pick up poop that morning. Oteitani had chuckled and could barely contain his laughter as he watched her study it and think it was something else. It wasn't until he became convulsed with laughter that she realized something was wrong.

Her victory that day, however, was short lived. After she had succeeded at getting him in the water, Oteitani got out and picked her up and carried her in. It was on that day that she decided that if being submerged in water and spending a few hours soaking wet were the worst of her worries, she'd take it, and from that moment on, Ehnita began to embrace every moment that came her way.

Since the morning that she pushed him into the water, something had sparked between the two of them. When they got out of the water, still laughing at each other, Oteitani looked at her in a way that made her feel whole. There was an undeniable chemistry between them. She could hear Black Raven in her ear saying, *kariwasei;* this was indeed a new way of doing things for her… She was letting her heart lead.

"Why are you staring at me like that?"

"Like what?"

"I don't know, like—like you've never seen me before or something."

"I haven't. Not like this." Smiling as water dripped down his chest, Oteitani laughed. "Come, Sky Woman, let's go eat something."

"I'm going to gain too much weight over here. Why are you always trying to feed me? I won't be able to fit any of my clothes when I get back home."

"I want to feed you because you are too thin. You should eat more."

"I'm too thin? I didn't think that was possible. I've been told that I could afford to lose a pound or two."

"Whoever has told you this, it is they who have never seen you before."

It was like her heart stopped. He had seen her at what she once would have described as *her worst,* no makeup, no fine finishing to her hair, no bodice, no armor at all—he had seen beneath her beautiful and she felt spectacular.

In addition to working with the women from the tribe washing clothes in the morning, Ehnita joined in on the food preparation in the late morning. Initially she was disturbed by the wild game that was broken down by the men and prepared by the women, but her discontent was quickly overshadowed by the intense warmth and care that went into the production from start to finish; there was so much love and attentiveness that went into how the animal was treated, Ehnita was completely astonished. She'd seen theatrical table side service in the past, but all the chefs she'd previously watched paled in comparison to these women and their diligence and creativity. By the time the women had finished with whatever animal had been brought to them, everyone in the tribe had something to eat, someone would have something new to wear or to sleep on, and the men would have several small, sharp objects to work with.

In the afternoons, when he wasn't off hunting or trapping, Ehnita spent her time with Oteitani and his nephew Ahanu. Unlike his uncle, Ahanu was thin, not as broad as Oteitani but almost as defined. His jet-black hair fell just beneath his shoulders, and although he was still young, as far as height went, he was almost shoulder to shoulder with Oteitani. There was a softness to his features that his uncle's face lacked. His big chestnut eyes were full of wonder and always appeared to sparkle when he spoke.

Ahanu reminded Ehnita a lot of herself at his age. He was smart, always alert and eager to learn. She could see so much potential in Ahanu, and just being near him excited her. He was constantly pestering Oteitani to translate questions about Ehnita's world. It made Ehnita wish she could take him with her when she went back home…whenever that might be. She was sure she'd get back home again. Her mother and Black Raven had made the trip more than once, and she was confident—if they could do it, so could she.

One afternoon, after having walked through the woods for nearly two hours, Oteitani, Ahanu, and Ehnita made their way over to the base of the waterfall to rest and for Oteitani to question Ahanu about what he had learned; the conversation, however, quickly turned into another question-and-answer session about Ehnita and her world.

"He wants to know what this name *Ana* means. This is his question, but I want to know as well."

Ehnita shrugged as she furrowed her brows at Oteitani. *Something classic and not so prehistoric sounding.* Ehnita could hear Barb's voice in her head. It had been so long since she had overheard Barb's comment to Martin about her name that she had almost forgotten the real reason she asked people to call her Ana. "It doesn't mean anything, I don't think. It just sounds nice."

"You give yourself a name with no meaning instead of using the name your mother chose for you?"

"Well, it's not like anyone in my world knows what my name means anyway. Ana or Anita, it's just easier this way, and besides, it all sounds the same anyway—kind of."

Ahanu looked at Oteitani, whose face had suddenly grown somber. "But it's not the same. Your mother gave you this name for a reason. Your name is more than just what you are called; it is who you are."

"I don't see it that way."

Letting his head fall briefly, he breathed deeply and shut his eyes. Oteitani was silent. Ahanu didn't understand the exchange that had not been translated to him, but very much understood the despair in Oteitani's current being. He, too, let his head drop in dismay. After a moment, Oteitani slowly turned his head to face Ehnita and opened his eyes. "I am not sure you see anything."

An image of Black Raven quickly came to Ehnita's mind as she looked across the water, trying to see through the mist and get a glimpse of the cabin she knew wasn't going to appear on the other side.

"You don't get it. You're used to it here. You like it here because you've never known anything else. Not everything has to mean something where I come from."

Sensing the turn the conversation had taken, Ehnita took a breath and put on a smile as she leaned forward toward Ahanu. "*You* would love it there. I was just like you when I was your age. I wanted to see everything and experience everything. I wanted more. I wanted better for myself. You would love it."

Ehnita stared at Oteitani, waiting for him to translate.

"I will not tell him this."

"Why not?"

"Because it is not good for him to hear. He has purpose. He has a direction. You say these things to confuse him, to make him lose himself. I will not do that."

Ehnita looked back at Ahanu and thought of her younger self. She had always felt alone, very much the stranger in a strange land, and she saw this same feeling in Ahanu, at least she thought she did. She always noticed him on his own or off to the side. When he wasn't with Oteitani, he was alone, and something inside Ehnita yearned to save him from his solitude because she knew firsthand how painful that isolation could be.

"Ahanu isn't like you, Oteitani. He wants more than this life."

"You do not even know yourself, yet you claim to now know my nephew." Rising to his feet as he looked down on her, Oteitani shook his head. "You speak of things that mean nothing in your world and names with no meaning—this is the life you would wish for him? To live in a world without purpose? Here he has everything because *we* are everything to everyone *for* everyone. He has more than you will ever know."

Not one to back down, Ehnita stood up in front of Oteitani. The fight for Ahanu's future, for Ehnita, had turned into a fight to defend the path that she had chosen for herself. "My world has so much more to offer him than you could ever offer him here. He could grow up to be somebody."

"He *is* someone already."

"That is not what I meant. You know exactly what I mean."

"Yes, I do. And yes, he is. Here he is somebody. He is someone who is loved, looked up to, looked after, and depended upon."

"Yes, but there is more to life than just that."

"Is there?"

"Yes."

"And this is why you left home?"

"Yes."

"And you are happy with the life that you have chosen where no one even knows your name or who you are?"

The fortitude inside of Ehnita suddenly fell flat.

"You choose your own path, Ehnita. You blame your mother for your life, but it is you who chose to leave, not her. She did not abandon you; she did not take you away from anything. She tried to bring you home. These things you have now to fill your life, to replace your people, to replace your mother; they will not care for you when you are sick. They will not feed you when you are hungry. They will not comfort you when you are scared. They cannot love you back."

* * *

Over the next two days, Ehnita made a conscious effort to be a little humbler when she was in Oteitani's company. Their previous fight had left a sour feeling in her stomach. She had argued with Ben many times before, but she never felt this way afterward. The thought of Oteitani being upset with her literally kept her up all night, but his smile the next morning raised her spirits and filled her with so much gratitude that she became determined to not offend him again.

The morning after their fight, she decided instead of trying to teach Ahanu things, she would be quiet and begin learning with him from Oteitani. Ehnita was pretty sure that the time she spent learning from Oteitani was the most amount of time he'd ever spent laughing in his entire life. It was certainly the most time she'd ever laughed in hers.

During these afternoon lessons, Ehnita tried her best to keep up, but if Oteitani and Ahanu were running side by side, she was usually running behind them. Where they leapt, she tripped. No matter what the task was, they gracefully got through it while Ehnita stumbled, sank, and bumped into everything. However, no matter how far behind she was, Oteitani was always there to catch her before she fell, and always just in time to pull her up before she sank.

She truly enjoyed all the physical activity and was truly interested in all the things she'd been learning, but it didn't stop her from answering the many questions Ahanu had about her world; neither did it stop Ehnita from subtly dropping hints to Oteitani that Ahanu would be better off going back with her. That is until one day when the questions stopped.

Ahanu's sudden about-face bothered Ehnita. His acute disinterest in all the things that she was excited to share with him hurt her feelings in an unwelcomed and unexpected way. When she tried to reengage him in conversations about her world and tell him all about five-star restaurants, fancy cars, and tailored suits, he only looked to Oteitani more often and with more intensity about whatever it was he was supposed to be learning that day. Each time his eyes looked at her as she spoke, she could hear the sound of Barb's laughter echoing in her ears.

Two days had passed since Ahanu's interest seemed to have vanished, and Ehnita's desire to know why was beginning to get the best of her. She decided that morning that she would find out the reason why. Ehnita spent half the morning going over in her mind what she would say and how she would say it. She wanted to speak with Ahanu directly, but since she couldn't, she made sure she chose her words carefully so as to not upset Oteitani. She was eager to begin her questioning but found she had no choice but to wait because her translator was nowhere to be found. It wasn't until early afternoon when she finally caught sight of him.

With her hands planted firmly on her hips, she stomped over to the man she'd been waiting to see all day. She was already irritated about Ahanu; now she was irritated that Oteitani had made her wait so long to tell him about it...not that they had planned to see each other that morning. Ehnita still felt as if she'd been made to wait on purpose, and she didn't appreciate it at all.

"Hey, I looked for you this morning. Where were you?"

"Preparing."

"Preparing for what?" Ehnita sat on the ground next to the cluttered bench where Oteitani sat sharpening his knife.

"Preparing to take Ahanu on his journey."

"Where's he going?"

"To find his manhood."

"And where exactly does he go to pick that up?"

"Into the woods."

Feeling a bit as if she'd entered the conversation somewhere in the middle, Ehnita took a step back mentally and quietly went over everything that had just been said.

"I don't understand."

After intently scrutinizing his handiwork by eye, Oteitani dabbed at the blade with his finger to test the sharpness.

"Ahanu has reached the age where he is no longer looked at as a child. I will take him into the woods, where he will stay and find the man he is to be."

"You're gonna leave him in the middle of the woods? Are you serious? He's just a kid."

Reaching for his satchel, Oteitani shook his head. "You would not understand."

"Understand what? Please explain to me how abandoning a child in the middle of the woods is going to help him become a man."

"He is not a child."

"He is not a man."

Frustration crept up Oteitani's neck and straightened his spine. "Here, manhood is something that is earned. Ahanu will go into the woods and learn how to survive on his own, and he will, as we all have. As I have. He will do this on his own, but he will never be abandoned."

"So, you'll be there with him?"

"I will not."

"Then you are abandoning him in the woods."

"It is not the same thing."

"Yes, it is."

* * *

What was to be a joyous day and proud moment had quickly turned sour. Not only was Oteitani offended by Ehnita's inaccurate interpretation of this important ritual, but he was also filled with resentment at her audacity to steal his pride for the act he was about to perform.

"You who abandoned your mother has no right to judge. We do this *for* Ahanu, not to hurt him."

"Now you're saying I abandoned my mother? That I hurt her? You didn't even know my mother."

"Neither did you."

For a moment, words eluded her. But indignation stepped in front of rationale and drove Ehnita into a fit. After kicking over the small pot at Oteitani's side, she threw her hands up in frustration and angrily paced around in circles.

"I did not abandon my mother! Is this why Ahanu stopped asking me questions about the other side?"

"He stopped asking questions because he no longer wanted to hear the answers."

"And what is that supposed to mean?"

"It means exactly as I have said. He no longer wants to hear of a world where his people do not exist, not in the way he knows we can. A small part of what we have now would never be enough for him. It would never be enough for any of us."

"And he could have more than that. He wouldn't be confined to the reservation."

"Here, there is no reservation. Only you cannot see that. You only see what you think *should* be, and for you that means destruction. That means tearing things apart. It means less earth, less soul, and no meaning. You say he will love it there, but he has love here, and that is what is important to him. He has chosen his path; he will not walk yours with you just so that you do not have to walk it alone anymore."

While Ehnita had always made her intentions clear—that she wanted to go home—a small part of Oteitani had been hoping that she would change her mind, that she would choose another path and stay there with the tribe, stay with him. That hope was now devastated, and Oteitani was not only offended, but he was hurt. He was also very angry and beyond insulted. Oteitani threw his satchel to the ground and kicked the dirt at his feet off to the side.

"Perhaps it is you I need to bring into the woods, Ehnita, so that you can stop behaving like such a child."

"Me? *I'm* acting like a child? You're the one name calling and throwing around insults."

"It is truth."

"It is not." Arms folded in petulance, Ehnita looked around, seemingly disgusted and annoyed with everything she saw. "I don't know why I'm bothering trying to explain myself to you, you prehistoric, chauvinistic—savage! I don't even know why I'm here. What exactly am I supposed to see—"

Exhaustion and sorrow filled Oteitani's chest. "You have seen exactly what you always have seen…that we are nothing more than savages. This is what you see. This is what your world teaches you."

"I want to go home."

"And you should. You do not belong here."

Unwilling to yield, Ehnita stomped her foot and let her hands fall by her sides. "I won't be made to feel bad because I wanted more for myself. I've worked hard for everything that I have, and I did it all on my own. You're right, I don't belong here. I'm better than this place."

"Then go. Find your own way home. I have more important things to do today than to indulge you in your childish behavior. Ahanu waits for me. I will not abandon him now when he needs me the most and spend any more time with someone who needs no one and who thinks of no one but herself."

"That's fine. I don't need you to find my way back home. I got here on my own. I can get back the same way."

"And this is why you will never understand Ahanu's journey. He may not yet be a man, but he is not childish enough to believe that he needs no one. Someone will always be there guiding him, whether he can see them or not. He knows that he is never alone."

Before she could respond, Oteitani had picked up the scattered items Ehnita had kicked across the ground and was now walking away from her.

* * *

Ehnita wanted to scream. She wanted to run behind him and tell him off. Instead, after a few moments of huffing and puffing in one place, she turned in the opposite direction and began walking full steam ahead.

Determined to prove herself superior in any way she could, she decided that once she left, she would not turn around. When she got back to the base of the waterfall, she was nearly out of breath from all the huffing and puffing she did on her journey; sweat stung her eyes as she stared at the wall of water in front of her and silently commanded it to stop.

"I can do this. I can figure this out."

Perhaps going through the water would get her back to the other side, get her back in front of the water-worn, barely moist wall she'd looked at so many times before when visiting Black Raven. As she climbed over the wet rocks and the cool mist from the water covered her face, her determination grew stronger and stronger with each step.

"I can do this. I can fix this."

At the edge of the cave where she once stood with Oteitani, she thought back to that afternoon and found herself beginning to soften, but the sound of the rushing water pulled her from memories, and she quickly shook off any notion of going back. In a sudden fit of rage, she charged at the water, at the memory of the man who had once brought her so much joy. As she smacked at the wet rocks, she lost her footing. Completely off balance, with both her arms stretched out, Ehnita's hands found the wall of the cave before she fell forward.

"Wake the hell up! You do not belong here!"

When the moment of blinding rage was gone, so was the falling water. The water had stopped, quiet had filled the space where it once was, and a large, damp, cold stone looked back at her as if it knew something she did not. As she stepped back away from the wall, she looked around and could see trees, but there was no forest, not like it was before. The trees were there, but now they were all scattered, where a moment ago they were stacked.

Overwhelmed with excitement, Ehnita turned and ran out of the cave and stood at the edge of stream. She looked across the water and she could see it; she could see Black Raven's cabin in the distance. She could see the trail that she had walked weeks ago, the trail that led to Wes's office. She'd done it.

Filled with pride, she turned her head very decidedly and looked up at the top of the waterfall and smiled at the bridge that hung just above her.

"Finally."

Turning toward the trail behind her, Ehnita quickly made her way back up the path that led to the bridge and walked across to the other side.

Right there where she had left it almost two full weeks ago was her car. After gently touching the hood, she ran up the stairs to Wes's office.

In his office, sitting behind his desk eating, surprised by her arrival, Wes quickly swallowed the large bite of food that he'd just put in his mouth.

"Ehnita. You're back."

"Yes. Finally."

"How are you? Please, have a seat."

Before Wes could fully get up from his chair, Ehnita's hands were up in protest as she shook her head. "No, I won't be here long. I just need my phone and if you could open my car door for me, please. I left my keys in—I left my keys, but I have a spare inside my center console. So, if you could just—you know."

"Of course I will. But please, sit and relax a minute. You look—"

"A mess. I know. I look a mess."

"No. Not a mess but you look drained."

"Yeah, that too. I'm definitely feeling very drained. But no, I really can't stay. I just need my phone and for you to open my car door so that I can go home."

"Of course." After handing over her phone, Wes went to the closet by his desk and retrieved a long toolbox. "Black Raven has been waiting for you. Have you seen him?"

"No."

Ehnita's terse response left no room for dialogue. Sensing her unfavorable mood, Wes nodded as he quietly walked around her and made his way outside to her car. It took him less than five minutes to get her car door open, and it took Ehnita less than that to retrieve her spare key from the console, start her car, and take off—all without saying thank you or goodbye.

Chapter Nineteen

By five o'clock Friday evening, Ehnita was finally home. As soon as she stepped inside her condo, she immediately went to her bathroom and turned on the shower. Before undressing she looked at herself in the mirror and stared at her wild hair and natural face. She stared at her reflection until steam from the hot water fogged up the mirror. She felt numb; she was finally home and yet she never felt so lost. She didn't recognize herself, and she was relieved when the fog finally made her disappear.

After an hour-long shower, Ehnita stood in her kitchen in a fresh pair of satin pajamas and slowly sipped a large glass of her favorite red wine as she powered on her phone. Her phone and her wine were both proving somewhat disappointing that evening. The wine was the last bottle she had of her favorites, and she was reluctant to open it but, in the end, considered her return home a worthy enough reason to celebrate. But the wine didn't taste the same. Her phone, which seemed to take forever to power on, only contained one message. After two weeks of being MIA, she had only one message.

"Hello?"

"Hey, beautiful, what's going on?"

"*What's going on*? That's all you have to say to me, Ben? After two weeks? No, *are you okay? Where ya been?* Just, *what's going on*?"

"What's wrong with you?"

After refilling her wineglass for the third time, Ehnita took a seat on her sofa and stared out at the night sky.

"Nothing's wrong with me, Ben. What's wrong with you? You don't see or hear from me in two weeks and you're not at all concerned? You didn't look for me—nothing?"

"I left you a message."

"Yes, you did. *A* message, a single message, as in one. You left a single message after not seeing or hearing from me in two weeks."

"Look, I don't understand why you're so upset. I figured you went back out to the reservation to spend some time with that Raven guy. I called and left you a message to call me back and let me know how things were going, which you didn't do by the way. And now you're mad at me?"

"I'm not mad."

"Then what's the problem?"

"Nothing. There's no problem."

"So, how did things go up there? Is everybody on board to sign?"

In the quiet of her apartment, Ehnita felt unbalanced. She was glad she was home, but it was only then that she realized she was the only one happy about her return. Her dog barely lifted his head from the pillow when she walked in, luckily the spoiled pooch had an excellent dog walker who tended to him during the week, otherwise had his care been left to the tender mercies of Ben, Ehnita would have returned to a devastating situation. Barb hadn't left a message. Ben had only left one. No one noticed her absence or missed her while she was gone, and no was waiting for her to come back. There would be no celebration here for her return.

"Look, Ben, it's been a long day, and I'm pretty tired. Let's say we meet up for dinner or something on Sunday night and we can talk."

"Okay, sounds good to me. Later, babe."

When Saturday came Ehnita decided to spend the entire morning at her favorite salon. She got steamed, stretched, rubbed, washed, blown out, curled, and polished. After the salon she spent several hours shopping and purchasing various unnecessary items just because she could. She even made a point to go into several stores she had visited in the past and refused to buy from because the items were too expensive in her opinion back then. But they weren't today; today she bought them all just because she could. Nothing had changed about them, not the fabric, not their value, not even her opinion on the price. What had changed was Ehnita's attitude. She felt she deserved the overpriced items; she felt they made a statement about who she was and how people should see her.

By one thirty that afternoon, Ehnita was back in her apartment, alone, sitting on her couch all glammed up and surrounded by a sea of overpriced, nonessential items. She even stopped on her way home and picked up the most expensive and highly decorated platter of sushi she could buy. She was surrounded by all the things she'd been wanting and talking about for days. She finally had it all right there in front of her, and much to her surprise, she couldn't have felt more ambivalent about it all.

Confused by the unexpected knock at the door, Ehnita was excited to have company that evening. She quickly made her way toward the door to see who her guest might be.

"Who is it?"

"It's me, Wes."

"Wes?"

Sure enough, standing on the other side of her doorway with a smile on his face, happy to see her again, was Wes.

"Hello, sister. I hope you don't mind me stopping by like this, but I wanted to check on you and make sure you were doing okay."

"No. I don't mind at all. Please, come in."

As they both began to sit down across from one another in the living room, Ehnita caught herself just before she was seated. "Can I get you something to drink, Wes? I've got juice, water, and wine."

"Water would be great, thank you."

When she returned from the kitchen with the water, she immediately noticed a wooden box that she hadn't seen Wes bring in with him but that was now placed in front of him on her coffee table right next to the overpriced, untouched platter of sushi.

"Here you go."

After handing him the water, Ehnita fingered the skillfully crafted box, admiring its intricate detail. "What's this?"

"This is for you."

"Oh no, Wes, you didn't have to get me anything."

"I didn't. What I meant to say is, this is yours. Your mother left it with Black Raven, and he asked me to bring it to you."

"Why didn't he just give it to me himself?"

"When you came back you didn't go to his house to see him, so I went down to his cabin to let him know that you had returned safely. He gave me the box to give to you."

"But why now? Why not give it to me himself one of the many other times I went there to see him?"

"Sister, I do not know."

Ehnita leaned forward and rested the box back on the coffee table and gently ran her fingers against the raised detail one final time before she lifted the lid. Inside the box were papers; they looked like the same papers that were in the box she'd gotten from Barb's house that contained the last of her mother's effects...or what she thought were the last of her mother's effects.

"I think I've seen these already. I don't know what they say."

Wes smiled and nodded. "Title paperwork. Ownership."

"Ownership to what?"

"To everything your mother owned. All of her land. She left it to you."

"Are you kidding me?" Ehnita's eyes widened with shock. "It's mine? All of it—it's mine?"

Staring at the paperwork in her hand in disbelief, she didn't know if she should laugh, cry, or scream. This whole time, right there in the box inside her office this whole time she had the one thing she needed to make the deal happen and she didn't even know it.

Back in her office when she first started researching the land, something inside of her told her that the answer was right there in front of her, staring her in the face. What she could never have imagined, though, was that it was her. She was in fact the answer to her own problem.

Despite knowing how sacred land was passed down, Ehnita never considered anything being passed down to her. Her sullen mood that evening had taken a drastic turn for the better. She was exuberant, not because of what she had just discovered she owned, but because she was right. Ben, Barb, and everyone else who doubted her, they were all wrong and she was right, and now she had proof.

While she couldn't understand the words that were written, she could appreciate the numbers, and the numbers were beyond anything she could have dreamed of.

"My mother owned all this land, and she left it all to me?"

Somewhat shaken by her reaction, Wes put his water down and sat up straight.

"Yes. I'm not sure exactly how much, but I do know your mother owned a decent amount of land, and as is our way, land is always passed down to another family member so that it is not sold. The papers you say you have seen already are probably the papers of who owned the land before it was passed to your mother."

"My God."

Ehnita couldn't hide her shock and confusion. "If she owned all this, then why did she… I mean, she died in that little trailer with nothing. Why didn't she ever build a house or sell it to someone else on the reservation, or something—anything? Why didn't she ever tell me?"

"That I do not know, sister. There is only one person I know who could probably answer that question for you."

"Black Raven."

Wes nodded. "Yes, Black Raven."

"You look amazing."

"Do I?" Ehnita knew she looked great. She'd spent the better part of the day before pampering herself to ensure that she did, and this evening she had on a twenty-five-hundred-dollar cocktail dress, four-hundred-dollar shoes, and a six-hundred-dollar curl job on her hair; she was hoping if she looked the part, she would be able to feel it too.

"Yes, you do. I can't believe it's been two weeks. I feel like we were just together a few days ago. I guess that's work life for you. You get so preoccupied, you lose track of time."

"Lose track of people" would have been a more appropriate statement. That Sunday evening, Ben sat across from Ehnita looking more refreshed than she did. His new clients had kept him busy since she'd been away, going out for drinks at night, golfing during the day, business talks in the sauna. It was a wonder how he could manage to fit in a haircut amidst all the chaos let alone have time to call her and leave her that single message.

"You look good too. Is that a new suit?"

"Yeah. My new client took me by this shop that's owned by a friend of his. I picked up a few things while I was there. Looks good, doesn't it? And it feels great too."

Sitting across from one another in the upscale restaurant, all dressed up, made Ehnita feel good. Ben's mere presence reminded her of everything she had been working for her whole life. "So, how have things been around the office? You have a date yet when you and your new client are expecting to break ground?"

"The office is pretty much the same. The only big thing right now is us and this reservation deal. So, did you make any headway? Were you able to get anyone to sign?"

Coyly sipping from her wineglass, Ehnita shot Ben a seductive glance and smiled. "Nope."

A sudden panic spread across Ben's face, quickly followed by an anxious, deranged grin. "What do you mean, no? You were gone for days, and you couldn't manage to get a single signature?"

The excitement was just too much for her. Nearly spilling her drink as she burst into laughter, Ehnita shook her head. "Nope, not one. And as it turns out, I don't need them anyway. I own over fifty acres of land on the other side of the waterfall, mere steps away from the area we were focusing on."

"Get out! Are you serious?"

"Yes."

Relieved and thrilled at the same time, Ben pushed his expensive plate of steak to the side and leaned forward on the table. "How is that possible? Why didn't you say anything before?"

"I didn't know before. It's a recent development. A very recent but very positive development."

"The partners are going to love us for this. You said it would happen, and you were right. I can't wait until Monday to tell everyone." Ben raised his glass in Ehnita's direction and smiled. "A toast to picture-perfect views and new corner offices."

"To views and offices." As her glass clinked against his, Ehnita sighed with satisfaction, but the sensation was short lived. The sound of their glasses touching echoed in her ears like the sound of faraway thunder and heavy rainfall, and suddenly her chest began to ache.

Chapter Twenty

"Hey, Barb. How are you?"

"Ana, love. I'm wonderful. What can I do for you today?"

"Oh nothing. I was just checking in with you to make sure things were okay. I was out of town the past two weeks. I wasn't sure if you'd tried to reach me or not, so I figured I'd check in."

Ehnita hadn't received any text messages or voicemails from Barb when her phone was finally charged. She scrolled through her call history as well; nothing there either. But still, Ehnita was somewhat confident that Barb had in fact attempted to reach out to her. She reasoned her battery might have been dead at the time, and she didn't want the woman to worry, so as soon as she was settled in her office at work on Monday, she gave her a call.

"Yes, dear, Martin and I are fine. I've been so busy with my charities the past several days, I haven't had time to think of much else. And I can't afford to fall behind on my charitable work, not when there are so many people depending on me. You know better than most how much good my projects can do for people. I mean, look how far you've come because of them. And Martin, he comes and goes as usual, always another meeting or convention."

For the first time ever, Ehnita had heard Barb, and she understood her clearly. She wasn't quite angry, but it was as if she'd just been woken up from a long sleep after a hard day. Ehnita wasn't her family; she was a project, a charity case, a *success* story. But the only one being celebrated in this scenario—the only successful person at the end of it all—was Barb. It was always Barb. Ehnita could finally see that, and in that understanding she managed to find a small piece of solace. She now understood why her mother left—she and Ehnita were never actually wanted. They didn't belong there. "Oh, okay. That's good. Glad to hear you two are doing well."

There was a brief moment of silence, which Barb quickly filled by clearing her throat. "Ehnita, sweetheart, did you need something? Is it your reservation project again? Do you need me to make another call?"

"Oh no, Barb, I've got that all worked out. Thanks to my mother, things are moving along great."

"Your mother?"

The fact that Barb didn't have the time to even think about Ehnita, let alone be worried about her, bothered Ehnita greatly. Barb's aloof and ambivalent attitude that day was not unusual, but it was the first time Ehnita had been troubled by it. She now knew she had placed value in a person who had never valued her and had never truly seen her—who didn't think enough of her to notice that she'd been missing, or care enough about her to miss her when she was gone…the way her mother had missed her all this time.

"Yes, my mother. She left me several acres of land on the reservation."

"She left you land? Your mother didn't own any land. How could she leave you land?"

"Oh no, Barb, she did own land, quite a bit of land actually. I verified the titles down at the clerk's office and everything."

"But your mother didn't have anything. From the time she came to us—we took her in with nothing, and she left with nothing."

Ehnita flinched as she looked down at the phone in her hand. She wasn't *nothing*; she was what her mother took when she left the suburbs and returned to the reservation. The only thing she wanted and the only thing that mattered. She took her daughter with her, and to Oneida, Ehnita was everything.

Ehnita was awake now, and it was as if she could hear and see everything her mother had seen and felt all those years living with Martin and Barb. While her mother had tried to take her away from it, shield her from it, Ehnita had run toward it. Her entire life she'd been chasing everything Barb never thought someone like her should have, and in doing so, she ran away from everything her mother had been trying to give her, which was so much more.

"My mother had a lot, actually. More than I could have ever known, most of which she gave away; her things, much like her heart, are scattered across the reservation. She gave without question or acknowledgment. So many families have come to me and thanked me for her kindness, and I'm happy to let them keep everything she gave because I know it's what she would have wanted."

"But she left *you* the land, right? Just you? You're not sharing it with anyone else, are you?"

As she turned in her chair to look out the window, Ehnita thought about the people living on the land already, the ones who were there and not there all at the same time. The land was indeed hers alone, but that was in name only. She was without question sharing it, and that knowledge left a burning sensation in her heart.

"The title is in my name only."

"That's wonderful, dear. Now you won't have to fight with those people about anything."

"You know what, Barb? I've got a call coming in. I'm going to have to run. You take care."

Ehnita hung up before Barb could say anything else. She'd never considered herself to be nor did she want to be looked at as Indigenous, but now being excluded from the community by someone who would never know what it meant to be part of it made all the hairs on the back of her neck stand up.

Before Ehnita could sit and stew in the indignation she felt simmering in her gut, her cell phone rang.

"Hello?"

"Ana. You need to get out here."

"Out where?"

"The reservation."

"Why are you at the reservation?"

In the distance Ehnita could hear Wes's voice, and he wasn't happy. There were other voices as well, and none of them sounded pleased with Ben's presence.

"I drove the developer up this morning to take a look at the land, and now some guy is here accusing us of trespassing. Just get up here, please. He's making all kinds of ridiculous threats, and our client is not happy. It's turning into a real mess."

"What? Why would you do that? Why would you... Why, Ben? Just—why?"

"Ana! I don't have time for this. Just get up here."

Typically, Ehnita didn't speed on the highway, but today she managed to reach the reservation in half the time it normally took her to get there. Today she drove fast; today she raced to her destination and surpassed every mile-per-hour restriction along her route.

As she got out of her car in front of the sheriff's office, she could hear voices in the distance coming from behind the building.

Ehnita nearly tripped over her own feet when she saw the fifteen people who were gathered outside the building and facing off with her client.

"I'm here." Panicked and nearly out of breath as she turned the corner, Ehnita offered a nervous smile and a wave, but no one seemed to notice her. "Hello." As if she were in the middle of a war and raising a peace sign, Ehnita waved back and forth as she approached. "I'm here. Hey. What's going on?"

"Ana, thank God, finally." Exasperated and visibly annoyed that it had taken her so long to get to his impromptu meeting, Ben stood with one hand on his hip and furiously rubbed at his temple with the other. "Ana, would you please tell these people that we're not trespassing."

"You were not invited, nor did you ask permission. In fact, you've been asked to leave several times, and you have not. That is the very definition of trespassing. You have no right to be here." As Wes spoke, he stepped closer toward Ben. His face was stern, and his body was rigid.

Peering around Wes's large, domineering frame, Ben looked at Ehnita, who stood silently, watching the exchange. Ben seemed confused as to why she was not stepping in. "Ana, would you tell him, please."

All heads began to turn in her direction, and all eyes began to focus on her. Ehnita took an apprehensive step back.

"Right… So, Wes, I can understand why you're upset, but this is all a misunderstanding."

"Explain it to us then, sister. Why are they here?"

"Well, the land—the land they came to see." She had the words, but for the first time ever, she found her head and her heart in conflict. Where her mind was leading, her heart would not follow.

"It's Ana's land!" Ben had finally had enough of Ehnita's stalling and blurted out what she could not say. "It's her land. And she is selling it to our client. So, you see, we *do* have a right to be here. In fact, we have *more* right than you do."

Ehnita cringed as the last of Ben's words fell from his mouth. Trying to quiet the storm before it came, she rushed over between the two men with her hands up facing Wes.

"He didn't mean it like that. He just meant—"

"What did he mean, sister? What?"

"Wes, please let me explain."

"Explain what? How you intend to sell our land? How you are trying to force us out? Take what little we have left and give it to those who have already taken too much? Is this what you are trying to explain, *Ana*?"

As if she'd just been shot at point-blank range, Ehnita grabbed her chest and went completely silent, tears filling her eyes. But she was determined not to let the situation get any more out of hand than it was, and so she took a breath and lifted her chin and readied herself to offer her defense.

"Wes, you have to understand—" Still the words would not come out. *This is my land* felt so untrue, so fraudulent that it pained her to say them; so, she didn't.

Moving slowly from the flock of people who stood behind Wes, Black Raven approached her. Once Black Raven was shoulder to shoulder with Wes, he stopped and sighed and slowly hung his head. Despite the slight grin on his lips, Ehnita knew in her soul he was anything but fine. He was far from happy about anything. The despair Black Raven felt in that moment was palpable.

"This is your land, Moon. We will go now."

"No. Black Raven, please. Please let me explain. I'm not trying to hurt anyone." Her voice cracked as she pled with him not to leave, but it was too late; everyone's backs were already turned. Shame filled every inch of Ehnita's body.

Ben looked at Ehnita and shook his head in dismay before turning to face the developer. "Finally, thank God, they're gone. I am so sorry, sir. I promise, you will not have to deal with this again."

As Ben apologized to their client, Ehnita stood with her back facing them and watched Black Raven, Wes, and the rest of the group walk away. Once they were out of sight, she took a couple of deep breaths, put a smile on her face, turned around, and shook hands with her future buyer.

After Ehnita had apologized to their client, Ben quickly turned his back on her and left the reservation laughing with their future buyer…he didn't even turn around to wave goodbye to her as she watched them drive away.

Ehnita got back into her car and left. Instead of heading back to work, she drove home. The ride felt like it took three times as long as the ride up there did. She drove in silence with only her shame and the sound of her mother's heart breaking in her ears to keep her company.

Several hours after the ordeal at the reservation, alone in her living room and now on her second bottle of wine, Ehnita thought about her mother and how as a daughter, she never had to try to make her mother proud of her; her mother always just was. Except today. Today Ehnita knew she disappointed her mother, and the image of her mother's crying face stood out so vividly in her mind that she couldn't stand it, and so she drank.

It was almost nine that evening when Ben showed up breathing and sighing as if he had had one of the roughest days of his life. "Hey, babe. Where'd you get off to this afternoon?"

Ben picked up one of the empty wine bottles from the coffee table and shook it as he raised an eyebrow at Ehnita. "So, is this why you didn't come back to the office? You've been celebrating all afternoon?"

Ben plopped down on the opposite end of the sofa, looking very pleased with himself as he stared back at Ehnita.

"The developer loved the views from the new site. He can't wait to get started. We're looking for a better route now to get to the other side so that we don't have to keep driving through the reservation, not to mention crossing the bridge. That thing's a death trap. That'll probably be the first thing they cut down."

"No."

"What do you mean, *no?* Have you seen the rickety old thing? Someone's going to get hurt, and since it connects both properties, both the reservation and our client would be liable. It would be a litigation nightmare."

The thought of the bridge being demolished down sent a sober chill up Ehnita's spine. She closed her drunken eyes and thought about Tatanka, and she knew in that moment that this— this was what Tatanka had been talking about. This was the torture he wanted no one to have. As she shut her eyes again and tried to block out the pain, the only thing she could see in the darkness of her mind was Oteitani's face looking back at her.

"No one's taking down the bridge."

"Ana, be reasonable—"

"No! I said no."

Ben watched as Ehnita left the living room and stumbled down the hallway to her bedroom. He'd never seen her behave in such a way before and was somewhat amused. He chalked up her resistance to his bridge idea to too much wine. Deciding he couldn't reason with her in that moment, he picked up the remote and clicked on the TV as he shook his head and laughed.

Chapter Twenty-One

Over the next two days, Ehnita read and reread the sale proposal from her buyer, who also happened to be her client. Since their ill-planned meeting at the reservation, Ehnita had decided not to go back to the office, but instead she worked from home. These days, her bosses let her do pretty much whatever she wanted; they were over the moon about her land rights and being that much closer to landing the largest deal in the firm's history. Aside from his work as a glorified chauffeur, Ben contributed very little to the project, but his posturing said otherwise. And because of that, the partners now treated him as if he walked on water.

That Wednesday morning, after a shower, instead of going through the sale proposal for the umpteenth time, Ehnita sat on her bed with the small box of her mother's things. As she touched the stones inside, she remembered the afternoons she spent by the water with the women from the tribe, washing clothes, humming, and laughing with each other. She smiled at the memory, and her fingers found their way to the photo of her mother and Black Raven. Overcome with the desire to know more, she quickly put her still-wet hair up into a loose bun, threw on a pair of jeans and a gray T-shirt, stuck her feet into some posh ballet slippers, and headed out the door.

At the reservation, she got out of her car as quickly as she could. She felt very much like a criminal jogging past the sheriff's office, trying to stay out of sight. She was ashamed and could still feel the sting from the last words Wes had spoken to her.

"Good morning, Moon."

Sitting on his porch, staring out across the water, Black Raven slowly let his hand rise and fall on the armrest of his rocker.

"Hey. I hope I'm not bothering you by just showing up like this."

"No."

As she sat in the chair next to his, the same chair she dragged next to his so many weeks ago, she unintentionally and unexpectedly let out a slight whimper. "Why didn't you ever tell me who you were?"

"You never asked."

"Why would I ask you something like that? Why would my mother not tell me? Why—why did we never meet before when I was young?"

"Would it have changed anything? Would you have stayed if you knew?"

She couldn't lie and she wasn't going to insult him by pretending. "No. I still would have left. But someone should have told me."

"Why?"

"Because I have a right to know."

Anger was easier than sorrow. Ehnita felt comfortable in this attitude, and she wanted to hold onto the feeling for as long as she could.

"You are right, Moon. We should have told you many things. Your mother, she tried many times to get you to listen to the most important things, but you could never hear." Black Raven took his eyes off the water and looked at Ehnita briefly before dropping his head and shaking it in despair. "She tried so many times."

"When? What? What did she try to tell me?" Furrowing her brows, she slumped down in her chair, trying to remember a moment when her mother had come to her to tell her something. The harder she thought, the louder the voice in her head got. *Come listen to the earth.* Her mother's pleading voice went off like a car alarm in her head. Ehnita grabbed at her chest as she remembered her response to her mother, the day before she left the reservation.

"Why, Mama? So I can be like you? Some crazy old woman with nothing, talking to myself?" She hadn't seen it when she said it, but now she could see her mother's heart breaking as she chastised her.

"I didn't understand what she was trying to tell me."

Black Raven nodded. "You did not want to understand. You wanted only to go away. To be away from her. To be away from here."

"She should have tried harder."

"And what could she have said? How do you tell someone about a place they cannot see? She knew the only way you would believe her is if you could see it for yourself. Only, she could not make you see, so she tried to get you to listen. To listen to the earth. Listen to your people."

"That's what she wanted me to hear? She could hear them?"

Sitting straight up in her chair, her eyes focused across the water, Ehnita searched for signs of life. "Are they here now? Can you hear them?"

Smiling with his eyes closed, Black Raven nodded. A surge of adrenaline shot through Ehnita's veins, and she shut her eyes tightly as she tried to focus in on the voices she missed hearing and longed to hear again. She was desperate to hear the songs that were sung in the language she did not understand but still felt so much like home.

Disappointed, she opened her eyes and cast them downward. "I can't hear them. I can't hear anything."

"They are there, Sky Woman."

It was as if he reached his hand into her chest and gave her heart a squeeze. Hopeful once again, she sat back up and with her eyes filled with tears, she smiled at Black Raven. Oteitani was the first and only person who had ever called her by that name.

"Me? You can hear them talking about me?"

"They search for you."

"For me?"

"Yes. Their voices call out trying to find you, to bring you home."

Ehnita sat in the bliss that was her newfound awareness…she was missed; she was being searched for and worried about. She stayed there sharing peaceful silence with Black Raven until the sun had crested and began making its descent.

When she finally made her way back up the path and was standing in front of her car, she decided she couldn't sneak away the same way she snuck in. She had always stopped and spoken to Wes when she didn't want to, and today she wanted to, and she hadn't. She didn't want to make another mistake by leaving without seeing him that day at all.

"Hey, can I come in?"

Ehnita waited with her hand on the doorknob, bracing herself to hear the words *No, get out*, words she felt she deserved to hear, but those words never came.

"You can come in."

She could hear the invitation, but she couldn't feel it. "Wes, I'm sorry."

With his eyes on his paperwork in front of him, he barely acknowledged Ehnita's apology. "Yeah."

"Really, Wes, I am. I didn't know they were coming up here. I would have called you first. I would have—"

"You would have what? You would have had more time to think of a story to tell me?"

On the edge of her seat, her hands in prayer position and tucked between her legs, Ehnita took a shaky breath as she leaned forward, trying to get Wes to look at her. "I swear, it's not like that, Wes. I was still going through all the paperwork when Ben called me saying they were up here. I was searching for a solution where everyone could come out winners. I wasn't trying to take anything away from anyone. I wasn't trying to hurt anyone, I promise."

"And what solution did you come up with where we could all win after we here have already lost? This place has never been good enough for you, I know that. But for us, it's home."

"You're right and I'm sorry. I never gave this place a chance. I was so afraid of becoming my mother, who, as it turns out, I didn't know at all. But anyway, I fought so hard against all things related to my mom, the reservation, the people, the culture, all of it. I didn't want any part of it. So I never got the chance to truly see what was here. And that's my own fault."

Confused and saddened by her statement, Wes softened, slightly.

"Why?"

"I don't know. I guess I've always felt that I was never enough *because* I was Indigenous, and I decided the only way to fix that was not to be."

"How can you not be who you are?"

Ehnita shrugged and shook her head. "I don't know. I'm still trying to figure that one out. I still don't feel like I quite measure up. The woman I call my second mother, she didn't even notice I was missing for two weeks, my fiancé didn't care I was gone, work didn't notice anything off, and my dog didn't even care when I came back home."

"If it makes you feel better to know, Black Raven and I waited for you. Every day you were gone, we kept an eye out for you."

"No, actually," Ehnita let out a sigh and halfhearted giggle, "it makes me feel worse. Why do you care so much, Wes? Why do you care at all? You hardly know me."

"You're family, sister. And this is your home."

The previous tension in the air had completely dissipated. As they chatted, Wes's face lit up when Ehnita told him about Oteitani, Tatanka and his wife, Ahanu, and the women from the tribe. While she spoke, Wes prepared her a small plate of food and poured her a cup of tea before settling back into his seat. His eyes sparkled as he listened intently.

"It's so different there. Imagine—if everything changed but also stayed the same…like we never had to *survive* anything because the levels of sorrow that we know of—the tragedies, the heartbreak…they never happened."

"Sometimes you have to sacrifice to gain. You left behind everything, sister, but you came back with so much more than what you had." Wes took a breath and smiled. "Wow, sister. I wish I could see it myself. It sounds amazing."

"It was. I wish you could too."

It was near eight o'clock that evening by the time Ehnita got back in her car to drive home. Despite working things out with Wes, something in her still didn't want to go. As she drove away, she watched the office fade away in her rearview mirror, and as the image got smaller and smaller, her chest got tighter and tighter, and her mind filled with regret.

Chapter Twenty-Two

Thursday morning, after taking her dog, Posh, for a walk, Ehnita was still craving more of the feeling she had when she was talking to Wes the night before, and so she decided to take the day off work and bring her dog with her on a drive up to the reservation.

A certain calm filled her as arrived on the land and drove through the property. She couldn't help but smile the closer she got to her destination. Today, unlike all the other days she'd visited, she drove past the street that led to the sheriff's office and instead drove straight to Auntie Layla's house and parked her car on the street.

"Good morning, Auntie."

"Good morning, Ehnita. Come in, come in. And who is this?"

More alert and energized than she'd ever seen him before, Posh ran straight past Layla and into the kitchen and began looking around.

"That's Posh."

"I didn't know you had a dog."

"Yeah, I've had him for about a year and a half now. I got him when he was six months old, I think."

They followed Posh into the kitchen, and Ehnita looked around as they passed through the living room. Amongst the various family photos and knickknacks that cluttered the large oak shelf pressed against the wall, Ehnita spotted a faded but still colorful piece of child's artwork that she recognized as her own.

"Auntie, is that the picture I drew when I was like seven years old?"

"Yes."

"Where did you get it?"

"Your mother gave it to me. She was so proud of you. She was always showing off your work and giving it to people."

"She did?" Ehnita chuckled and smiled as she stared at the picture. "It's terrible. Why did you keep it? You should have thrown it away."

"Never. You worked so hard on that picture. I will keep it always."

The sincerity in Layla's words humbled Ehnita as she looked at her and smiled.

"Now, my Ehnita, you will sit and have some food and tell me all about your journey."

"You know about that too."

"Of course I do. There are no secrets between my brother and me. Black Raven tells me everything, especially the journey of his one and only grandchild."

As Ehnita ate the smoked meat and fruit Layla laid out for her, she began her story by telling Layla about how she learned to fish and to dry out hides. She then recounted her time spent during the day with the women and how they picked fruit and berries; she told her about Oteitani and her harvesting plants for medicine with him.

"It all sounds so wonderful, my Ehnita. I would have loved to be there with you. I know your mother would have loved this too. She wanted so much to go back."

"Yeah, Black Raven said that too. Then why, Auntie, why did she leave in the first place?"

"Your father, Black Raven's only child, he died, and your mother was heartbroken. She got angry. She blamed the other side for not having there what we have here. She didn't believe it was his time. She felt as if he should have been saved, and that if he was here, he would have been. When your father's life was done, she got so angry, she left. Then when she came back to this side, she was still angry, and living on the reservation was just too much for her. So she ran away. She took you and she left. She was only sixteen, no money, no job, and out there on her own in the world being so young, it was too much for her to survive by herself. And having you made it impossible, and she fell into the system. This is how you ended up with the family that took you both in. Your mother lost her way, and I am grateful that the family took you both in, but your mother, she knew she was not on the right path and so she came home. She realized without direction she could never lead you, my Ehnita, to the truth of who you truly are and who you were meant to be. She could not do this unless she found herself again and made peace with what happened."

"So, my mother wasn't born there?"

"No."

"Then how did she know about it? How did she get there?"

Layla smiled as she took away the empty plate from in front of Ehnita.

"You must have been hungry."

After putting the plate in the sink, Layla quickly left the kitchen and returned with a brush. She stood behind Ehnita and hummed as she softly placed the tips of her fingers on Ehnita's forehead and tilted her head back and looked down at her and smiled. "You and I, we will make more to eat."

"Thank you, Auntie."

"No need to thank. This is what we do for family. Now, I will get everything ready and then I will tell you about your mother."

More to eat. The thought warmed her from the inside out. She'd been hungry ever since she returned home. Back to a world that was abundant in resources, where she didn't have to do it herself, where everything was precooked, portioned, and *ready to serve*; she found herself starving. She'd never felt fuller than after eating a bowl of berries she had picked and a piece of fish that she had caught. The food in the city didn't smell the same. It didn't taste the same. It didn't fill her. She was excited and grateful for the food that Layla had prepared, and she was eager to have more.

Quickly and thoughtfully, Layla bent down and gave Ehnita a quick kiss on the top of her head. "But first, I will brush your hair and braid it so that it does not get in the way."

As Layla brushed her hair, Ehnita shut her eyes and fell into the same place of serenity and calm that she'd fall into when it was her mother who would brush her hair. When Layla began to hum the same tune her mother used to in these moments, Ehnita opened her eyes and smiled.

"My mother used to hum that same song to me."

Pausing as she looked down at Ehnita, tilting her head back so that they could see each other's faces, Layla smiled. "Yes, and I used to hum it to her when I brushed her hair, just as my mother sang to me and her mother before her sang to her."

Without the curls, Ehnita's hair was a good three inches longer than it normally appeared to be. Usually, when her hair was curled, it would stop at the small of her back, but straight, in its natural state, her hair fell just below her butt. She was glad she never cut it. She had more pride in herself in that moment than she had when she walked across the stage at her college graduation.

With her hair now in one long braid, Ehnita headed to the counter and stood shoulder to shoulder with Layla.

"There now." Her hand under Ehnita's chin, Layla smiled at Ehnita before reaching over her shoulder and grabbing the braid so that she could tie a hairband around the end of it. Once the braid was secure and had been tossed back over Ehnita's shoulder, Layla took Ehnita's face into her hands and smiled as she shook her head in disbelief. "So much like your mother."

Ehnita smiled back and placed her hands on top of Layla's. She felt somewhat giddy, and she was eager for more—more time, more songs, more love. "What are we making, Auntie?"

"Stew. You cut the potatoes."

As Ehnita peeled and chopped, Layla explained how she truly didn't know how Ehnita's mother had gotten to the other side; she didn't know how Black Raven came and went either. It was something inside of them, something inside their veins… something in their souls that brought them home.

"What about Mama's jewelry? I wore her earrings that you gave Wes to give to me. Could those have been what helped me travel?"

"Oh no, sweetheart. Those earrings came from the other side, but they did not get you there. She left them with Black Raven when she took you and left the other side. He begged her not to go, not to take you with her, but she wouldn't leave you there; so, she left the only other piece of your father that she had left, which were the jade stones he had given to her. It was a few years before Black Raven followed your mother and crossed back over to this side, but when he did, when he found your mother again, he returned to her what she had left with him. Your mother was grateful, but it made her sad to wear them, so she gave them to me. But I always thought that she should give them to you. You got to the other side not because of something that you wore on the outside but because of something you have on the inside. You inherited a gift. A wonderful gift."

"Can anyone else besides me and Black Raven travel?"

"Not that I know of. When I was younger, I used to hear stories of people who could live between both worlds, and I wanted so badly to go there myself back then. And then one day, I was looking around the woods across the bridge, and there he was. Black Raven. He stayed for a while, trying to convince your mother to bring you back home, but then he left again when he could not persuade her to. He stayed there for many, many years. Your mother did want to go, but she had only just returned home herself, and you were so angry. She didn't want to put you through any more changes just yet. She wanted you to get settled first. But you never did, and then too much time passed, and you were gone again."

Everything Layla had said about her was all fact—facts she couldn't deny or argue with. When she came to the reservation, she was angry and unsettled, and when she left, she was the same way. The thought of her mother dying, waiting on her to come back home, made Ehnita's heart hurt. And now with the knowledge that

Black Raven had been waiting for her too, it was almost more than she could bear.

"Why did he come back?"

"For you."

While the stew simmered away on the stove, Ehnita watched as Layla threw in pinches of this and pinches of that, which all went straight into a bowl of flour that she had now turned her attention to.

"Then why did he never come to look for me?"

"Because you didn't know yourself at that time that you were lost."

As she poured cream into the flour mixture, Layla sighed. "I never met my nephew, but I miss him all the same. Black Raven and I are not brother and sister by blood, but we are by spirit. Ever since the day I found him. And I am my brother's keeper, so I know, my Ehnita, I know how much he wanted to bring you home. He did not stay away because he was hiding; he stayed away because you were not yet ready. You are all that Black Raven has left of his son. He wanted to be here for you. Now, this place has become his home. He has purpose here. I'm happy that he's come back. I missed him while he was gone. But more importantly, he is the one who reminds us of all that we have forgotten of our people and our ways."

"Do you think he'll ever go back?"

"No. His life is here now. He enjoys passing down everything he learned growing up on the other side. He takes great pride in reestablishing our traditions and keeping them going. That is why he lives down there by the waterfall. He can hear them best from down there; he is able to feel as if he is still with them while also being here with us. He lives right on the line between heaven and earth."

"I can't hear them. Why can't I hear them?"

"I do not know." After placing a bowl of stew on the table, Layla went back into the living room, and this time she returned with a photo album. "Leave this bowl here. I will clean everything later. Come and sit down and eat your stew while the cakes are finishing in the oven. And look what I have for you. I have pictures of your mother here before she left for the other side and also some from when she finally returned home."

With each turn of the page, Ehnita's mother's smile appeared to get bigger and bigger. What Ehnita didn't realize was so did her own. As she sat slipping through the pages, she hadn't noticed that Layla stepped away to get her camera, and it wasn't until the flash went off that she realized she was sitting alone at the kitchen table.

"My mother looks so happy in all these pictures." As she smiled a tear fell from Ehnita's eye. "She must have been so disappointed in me."

"Disappointed? Never. She was so proud of you. You were her whole world."

"I wish I could have known her better. I feel like I don't know who she was at all, and I know that's my own fault. I wish I could tell her how sorry I am that I didn't get it back then. I didn't understand. I just want to tell her I'm sorry—and that I get it now. I get it."

Ehnita tried to smile through the tears that were streaming down her face. Layla put the camera down on the table and pulled her chair closer to Ehnita's until their knees were touching. She took Ehnita's hands into her own, smiled, and took a breath that persuaded Ehnita to do the same.

"You, Ehnita, were your mother's greatest joy. You both kept things from each other. This is why secrets are no good. There is fault on both sides, but none of that matters because of all the love that was shared between the two of you." Layla reached up and gently wiped the lingering tears on Ehnita's cheeks. "Even when you left, Ehnita, you would call your mother every day. My— how the two of you would fuss at each other on the phone." Layla chuckled. "But not a day passed that you did not speak to her. No matter how many miles away you were from one another, you were always together. And that is the truth. That is real."

The smell of the cake brought Posh running from the back room, where he'd been resting on some throw pillows. Ehnita couldn't help but laugh at the sight of him wagging his tiny little tail vigorously as he stood by the oven door, waiting for it to be opened.

"I think your dog is telling me the cake is done."

"I think so too. I never cook in my apartment. He's probably confused now about where food comes from. He's used to seeing bags and boxes."

Posh didn't get any cake, but he was satisfied with the few pieces of jerky Layla threw his way.

"Come now, my Ehnita, walk with me to bring some food to Wes."

"Okay. Auntie, why do you always cook for Wes?"

"Wes is a good man."

"Yes, I think he's a very good man. I was just wondering."

"I know what you mean, my Ehnita. I was not finished, my darling. Wes is a good man, and right now he does not have a good woman in his life to care for him. So, I step in and help out when I can. His mother has been gone a long time, and his father is disabled. Wes has taken care of him since he was very young, and now he takes care of the whole community too. I like to make sure he does not forget to take care of himself."

"That's sweet."

"For a while there, Black Raven and I thought there might be something with you two. But Wes has said that your heart is no longer yours to give away. Now, after hearing you speak of Oteitani, I see what he means, and I also see that he is right. You may be giving this Ben fellow your hand, but you have given Oteitani your heart."

As they walked together to Wes's office, Posh pranced alongside them, happier than Ehnita had ever seen him before.

After briefly visiting with Wes and dropping off his food, Ehnita said her farewells and she and Posh drove back to her condo. In the back seat, Posh looked as sad as Ehnita felt sitting up front, driving in silence, trying not to cry.

It was a little after seven that evening when she got back to her condo. Ben was already there waiting for her. Despite his relucatance to set a wedding date or simply give up his apartment and move in with her, Ben had no problem with taking Ehnita's key to her place and coming and going as he pleased.

"Finally, you're here, babe. I've been dying to go out and get some sushi. How quick can you get dressed?"

"I'm not hungry. I already ate."

"Ate where? Dressed like that?"

"Yes, dressed like this. My aunt's house. I ate at my aunt's house."

"What am I supposed to do? I've been waiting for you."

Waiting on her—it was a bit of a stretch; *relying on her* would have been a much more accurate statement. How else would he get a table at the best sushi place in town last minute? Ben treating Ehnita like a literal meal ticket didn't bother Ehnita; what bothered her was his blatant disregard for her feelings. He never cared enough to ask *why, when,* or *how* about anything going on in her life. Despite never having heard her name before that evening, he didn't care who Layla was, how they were related, or why Ehnita had gone to see her. He never even bothered to ask about what she found out about Black Raven and her mother. For all Ben knew, Black Raven was her father just as he had so wrongly assumed he was.

"I didn't ask you to wait, Ben, and you never called me to make plans. I don't know what you're going to do. Do whatever you want. Order takeout or something. I don't feel like sushi tonight. I'm gonna go and take a shower."

After standing under the pressure of her shower for almost an hour and still not feeling what she had hoped she would, Ehnita got out and dried off. She put on some satin blue pajamas and twisted her hair up into a towel to dry and walked back into the living room.

"So, what did you order?"

"Italian."

"Did you get me anything?"

"You said you already ate."

"I did, but still."

"But still what? It's not like you can't afford to miss a meal, Ana."

"It's not about the food, Ben. You didn't even think… Never mind."

Ben was obviously annoyed with Ehnita too, but he didn't care enough to continue the conversation with her, so, after a quick huff and shake of his head, he went back to eating his food and not paying her any attention.

Sitting on the opposite end of the sofa, with her knees pulled up to her chest, Ehnita looked at Ben and realized after not seeing him all day, she hadn't missed him at all.

"Posh. Posh, come here." With her hand dangling down from the sofa, Ehnita scooped up Posh and sat him in her lap.

"You shouldn't do that—play with the dog on the furniture. You'll get him thinking it's okay for him to sit up here."

"He's not sitting on the furniture; he's sitting on my lap."

"Same thing."

After making his feelings known about Posh, Ben went back to looking at Sports Center on TV. "Hey, did you go over the sales proposal yet and submit the paperwork?"

Ben's eyes were still on the TV, and Ehnita realized in that moment that Ben never looked at her when he spoke to her, and on the rare occasion he glanced her way, he never really saw her. He certainly didn't respect her. She realized something else that evening… She never felt lonelier than when they were alone together. Once again, her mother was right.

"Yeah, I looked at it. I'm tired. I'm going to bed."

After gently placing Posh down on his dog bed, Ehnita walked back into her bedroom, got in bed, and pulled the covers up closely around her neck. She must have truly been tired because no sooner than she'd shut her eyes, she was fast asleep.

"No!"

Shocked from her sleep by a dream she couldn't remember, Ehnita looked at the clock, which read one thirty, as she gasped for breath. In her dream, once again, she was falling into darkness, and she couldn't figure out why or how she got there.

"What is it, babe?"

Ben barely lifted one eyelid as he *checked* on Ehnita.

"Nothing, just a bad dream."

"Okay, well, go back to sleep."

Sitting up in the bed, Ehnita frowned as she looked down at Ben, who had already rolled over and gone back to sleep. In the darkness, in the quiet of the room, Ehnita could feel exactly what her mother had been saying; every inch of her heart ached with loneliness. Her eyes searched the room for the man who would have stayed up all night to catch any and every bad dream her mind could have conjured.

While the dream had shocked her, she wasn't actually afraid of it, but what she was afraid of was her reality, the sobering reality that this whole time, it was never her mother, Oneida, who needed to be saved from her life—it was her, it was Ehnita herself who needed rescue from her own. But her mother was gone, Oteitani was beyond her reach, and all she had left was everything that she had spent her entire life working for, which in that moment amounted to nothing, because it meant nothing to her now. It was all meaningless and offered no comfort.

Terrified and feeling more alone than she ever felt in her entire life, she couldn't go back to sleep. As she twisted her body around so that she could sit up and let her legs dangle off the side of the bed, she looked down and stared into the eyes of her concerned dog, who was the only soul that came to her rescue that evening. She flinched when she felt the sudden jerk of the comforter being snatched from underneath her by Ben's body as he rolled over in his sleep. As she glared at him in the darkness of her bedroom, she couldn't help but think, *I want to go home.* Unable to get the thought out of her mind, Ehnita jumped off the bed and scooped Posh up the floor, snatched her keys from the nightstand, and stuffed her feet into a pair of house slippers and left.

Ehnita's mind was blank for the first time in forever. That evening she was being led completely by her heart, and the ache in her chest brought her back to the reservation. Her movements were instinctive and without hesitation, and somehow in the darkness, she made her way down the trail behind Wes's office and safely across the bridge to the other side of the waterfall with Posh in her arms. Once she was at the base of the waterfall, she found the cave that she had entered before when she was there with Black Raven, and she frantically searched the area. Anxiety and frustration filled her chest as she tripped over rocks and smacked at the stone wall that once ran fiercely with water.

Like an explosion had gone off in his chest, Oteitani was startled awake by the sound of sadness, by the sound of Ehnita's panic and pain. Rushing from his teepee, he ran and gathered others to help him find her.

In the darkness, Oteitani, Ahanu, and several other men from the tribe searched and called out to Ehnita as they made their way to the waterfall. The sound of her sorrow grew stronger with each step Oteitani took. The sound of her hurt rolled across his heart the same way thunder roared across the sky. The men searched and called, but they could not find her. After hours of searching with no luck, the men he had brought with him eventually began to return to the village. They were tired and heartbroken that they could not find their lost family member. In the end it was just Oteitani in the cave at the base of the waterfall, refusing to give up. The sorrow he felt that evening literally brought Oteitani to his knees, and as he knelt there in the cave, he pressed his hand to the wall and shut his eyes and he prayed. He prayed all night… Alone in the darkness and the dampness of the cave, Oteitani stayed there on his knees all night, trying to pray Ehnita's pain away, hoping that she would once again find her way back home.

After putting Posh down along the water's edge, Ehnita ran frantically back and forth and in and out of the cave, calling for Oteitani and pleading with the sky to send her back. The legs of her pajamas were cut, and small patches were soaked in blood from when she'd fallen and injured herself.

Tired and emotionally drained, Ehnita crawled into the cave and leaned against the wall and rested her head on the cool rock. Confused and alone and feeling very lonely, she pulled her legs up to her chin and cried. She cried in a way she didn't know she could.

She cried for her mother, for Oteitani, for Wes and Black Raven; she cried for her father, who she never met; she cried because she wanted to go home.

The sound of footsteps, along with Posh's barking, snapped her out of her grief for a moment. Ehnita held her breath and cautiously turned to see who was approaching, and with the tiniest bit of hope in her heart, she looked up and prayed that it was him.

"Moon."

Black Raven looked down at her knowingly. He said her name and nothing else. There was nothing else to be said.

"Sister, are you okay? What are you doing here?" Seeing Ehnita in this state shocked and terrified Wes. As he rushed over to assess her injuries, he asked again and again if she was okay.

Not wanting Wes to worry, Ehnita looked at him and tried to smile. She tried to speak, but all she could do was cry. Her head rolled back against the wall, and her entire body heaved with sorrow.

Cautiously and as gently as he could, Wes scooped her up in his arms and carried her out of the cave.

Chapter Twenty-Three

Ehnita woke up on Friday morning to the sound of birds singing. Dust particles danced in the sun stream that crept through the thin-paned window of the cabin. At the foot of the bed, Posh popped his head up and stared at Ehnita, searching for confirmation that she was okay. After she sat up and reached down to give him a quick tousle behind the ear, Posh jumped down off the bed and scurried into the kitchen. With a quick stretch, Ehnita followed behind him.

"Good morning, Moon."

"Good morning."

"Sit down. Have some food."

On the kitchen table was a plate of scrambled eggs, fried potatoes, sausage, and a cup of coffee.

"How long have you been up?"

Black Raven sat down across from Ehnita with his cup of coffee and thoughtfully tapped the brim. "I have been up for a while. Your dog and I took a walk, and then I made breakfast when I came back."

Ehnita looked down at her potatoes and sausage and excitedly picked up her fork, ready to dig in, but she found herself suddenly overcome by the memory of smoked fish and she paused.

"I miss him."

Ehnita voice was barely above a whisper, but Black Raven had heard her loud and clear. He knew what she had said before the words had even come out of her mouth.

"I know. You want to go back. I know that too."

She wasn't angry or upset. She was deflated and confused, and in so much pain. Ehnita ate without tasting and moved without intention as she looked down at the plate blankly.

"Why? Why couldn't I go back?"

With her eyes opened as wide as the moon and tears sparkling like stars in the night, Ehnita looked at Black Raven with quivering lip as she tried desperately to cling to the hope that there was an explanation and, therefore, had to be a solution.

"It was not your time."

"Why not? When then? When will it be my time?"

"You only need to listen, Moon. Listen to the earth. You will hear it."

"Hear what?"

"Sounds of home."

A single tear fell from her face as she smiled. "I miss it. The sound of nothing and everything all at once—the wind and the water. You can actually hear *peace* over there. I can't hear it here. I can't hear it; I can't feel it. I can't—I feel like I can't breathe here anymore."

Once her plate was empty, Ehnita went to the sink to wash it. As she dried the plate, she looked out the window, hoping to see something that wasn't there, but what she could feel in her heart was there…water. She looked and listened for the sound and sight of rushing water that had never stopped running.

"Come, Moon, let's take a walk."

As they strolled together slowly, Posh ran ahead of them, joyfully running back and forth between the trees and Black Raven's legs. Posh was clearly at home here, and she envied the pooch. While they walked Ehnita shut her eyes and balled up her fist, desperately trying to pull sound from the silence.

Black Raven chuckled at the sight of Ehnita's intermittent straining. "You will hear nothing this way except the sounds of your own mind."

"How do you still hear it?"

"I hear it because I listen. The sound travels through me." Patting his chest and laughing as he laid his hand across his heart, he looked at Ehnita thoughtfully. "And here." With his other hand he placed two fingertips on the center of his forehead.

"Auntie Layla says you don't want to go back. Is that true?"

"My place is here, Moon. Heaven and earth have changed places for me more than once. I am happy where I am, right between the two."

"Why did you give me the title to the land?"

"Because it is yours. Your mother left it to you."

"Yes, but you know what my job wants to do to it. They want to destroy it."

"Aha, now you see destruction where you once saw improvement. Now you are beginning to see."

"Yeah, I guess I am. But what am I supposed to do? They're ready to start building."

"It is not their land to build on. It is yours."

Out of the corner of her eye, Ehnita could see Wes waving at them from a distance.

"Little sister, Black Raven, good morning."

Black Raven nodded and gave Wes a pat on the shoulder before he passed by and continued to follow behind Posh. Smiling, Ehnita reached up and gave Wes a hug. "Morning, Wes."

"Good morning. How are you feeling today?"

"I'm good. How about you?"

"I'm good. Better now that I know you're okay. I was worried."

"Wes, I'm sorry. I didn't mean to make you worry and to drag you out of your house this morning."

"It's okay, sister. As long as you are okay. It's fine."

"How did you know where I was?"

"One of the neighbors saw your car parked at the station. The car was still running, and the lights were on. They were concerned there might be an emergency, so they called me. I walked down to Black Raven's cabin first, and you weren't there, but he knew where you would be."

As they walked back toward the cabin together. Wes told Ehnita all about his plans to help the people on the reservation to find jobs and to get them the tools they needed to make the community stronger. He admitted some had been tempted to sell because of the money, but now no one would allow them to. The community had pulled together, and everyone was willing to sacrifice what they had to help those who didn't have enough.

They were setting up day cares to mind people's children while their parents were away and organizing carpools to drive people into the city to find work. They had a small group of young boys who would go to the scrapyards and gather items to help people repair their homes. They were holding fundraisers and selling jewelry and crafts. They were doing whatever they had to do to help each other out. It was during this planning that Wes met Rea, a woman just as passionate about the community as he was. By the way he spoke of her, Ehnita could tell Wes was lovestruck.

"Wow, Wes, I'm so happy for you."

"Well, we've only just started talking, so I guess we'll see where it goes. I really like her, though."

"Auntie Layla is going to be so excited for you."

"I know. She's tried to set me up so many times before, but it never worked out."

"Well, who knows, maybe Auntie will be catering your wedding sometime in the near future. That would make her very happy."

Sitting down on the steps of the cabin beside Wes, Ehnita stretched and then rested her elbows on the step behind her and she laughed.

"So, you were ready for a fight this whole time? And here I was thinking I was pulling you closer to my side. Quite the silent assassin you are. I never would have seen it coming, all this planning and strategizing you did against me."

Wes laughed as he leaned forward. "Yeah, I'm sorry, sister. I love you, truly, but this is home, and I will always fight for it. I will always find another way, you know? It's our home."

Ehnita smiled and nodded. "Yes, it is."

With her face pressed toward the sun and her heart pressed to the sky, Ehnita let her head hang back as she bathed in the peacefulness around her. There in that quiet moment, a sound she had been longing to hear rippled across her eardrums and sent shock waves through all of her senses.

"*Su—wee!*"

On her feet, smiling, she searched the tree line across the water; she couldn't see anyone, but she knew they were there.

Wes got up and stood next to her, his eyes squinting as he tried to see what Ehnita was so excited about.

"What is it? What are we looking for?"

Smiling but not taking her eyes off the trees across the water, Ehnita's heart raced. "Life. So much life, Wes."

Not wanting to be left out of the action, Posh ran up and stood in front of Ehnita and faced the water and scanned the shoreline. Black Raven quietly walked past the trio and took a seat on his porch. Humming softly to himself, he began to rock and slowly fill his pipe with tobacco. He looked at Ehnita and gave her a single nod before his whole face was surrounded by smoke clouds.

Hopeful and exhilarated, Ehnita got back up and walked up the steps and gave Black Raven a kiss on the cheek. With her hand on her heart, she smiled and nodded at him.

"I've gotta go. I'll be back." Running back toward the path with Posh jogging alongside her, Ehnita waved back at the two men. "Bye, Wes. Thanks again for everything. I'll be back soon, I promise."

Chapter Twenty-Five

When Ehnita returned home late Friday morning, Ben had already gone to work. She checked her cell phone to see if perhaps she had missed a call from him, but she hadn't and she really didn't care. After taking a quick shower, she threw on a pair of capri pants and a satin button-up shirt and then quickly tied her hair up into a bun and was out the door. She drove all the way to Barb's house to collect the rest of the items she had left behind. Small things that now meant everything to her. Things from her childhood... memories of her mother.

Though he had woken up in her condo without her, Ben had yet to call Ehnita and check on her. To be considerate, when she got home Friday morning, she called him, but she was sent to voicemail. When she woke up Saturday morning, she should have been tired, physically exhausted from all the running around that she had done the day before in the early hours of the morning at the reservation, and then spending half the day in Barb's garage, looking for pieces of her past, but she wasn't. Saturday morning, Ehnita woke up exhilarated.

After making herself breakfast, she took Posh for a walk in the park. Despite being a dog owner for over a year and living in a pet-friendly area, she'd never been to the dog park, which was right on the property where she lived. For over an hour Ehnita watched Posh run and play with other dogs. It amused her to see him like this. She'd always categorized him as a lazy house dog, but he wasn't; he had simply been in the wrong home. She could relate to the feeling.

After bringing Posh home, Ehnita went to her bedroom and gathered all her jewelry and carefully eyed each piece before placing it inside a small satin bag, everything except the crescent moon jewelry that had once belonged to her mother. The thin chain with the crescent moon pendant that she had found in the box, the ring and earrings that Auntie Layla had given to her, she took those out of the box and wore them.

Stop one, the jeweler. After some skillful negotiation on her part, Ehnita walked away with a check for over one hundred and fifty thousand dollars. She got much less than what she expected she would get from the engagement ring Ben had bought her, but it was okay because the jewelry she had purchased for herself more than made up for its worth.

Stop two, the art dealer. This stop put another eleven thousand in her pockets that day. Stop three was the bank. With both checks successfully deposited, she felt a great sense of accomplishment.

Once she was back home in her condo, standing in front of the mirror in her bedroom, she saw herself clearly for the first time. She caressed the crescent moon pendant between her fingers and thought of her mother and felt at peace with the decisions she had made that morning. For the first time in her life, thinking of her mother had brought her an unexpected and overwhelming sense of calm. Happy and grateful for this feeling, Ehnita took off her capris and put on the suede skirt from the box of her mother's things. She then quickly took the pins out of her hair and unraveled her bun and found she was comfortable and more confident than she had ever been when she was wearing a hundred-dollar dress, thousand-dollar shoes, layers of makeup, and layers upon layers of curls. She looked in the mirror and smiled, and after gazing at herself for a minute, she laughed. She'd never realized it before, but she looked a lot like Black Raven. If she'd seen herself like this before, no one would have had to tell her she was his grandchild. She would have already known.

The sound of her phone vibrating on the nightstand pulled her away from her thoughts.

"Hey, Wes."

"Hello, sister, I hope I'm not disturbing you."

"No. Not at all."

"I know you were just here yesterday, but we have a small issue here in my office. Would you mind driving up to help us out please?"

"Absolutely." It didn't matter what the issue was. She was going to drive up regardless. But as the call ended, Ehnita could hear Ben's voice in the background, which annoyed her and prompted her to move faster.

After jogging around her condo and grabbing a few items—some folders, her checkbook, and Posh's dog bed—Ehnita took her keys and called for Posh to follow her. She headed out the door.

She wasn't sure what to expect when she walked into the sheriff's office that afternoon. She knew Ben was there, but she was surprised to see their client along with one of the partners from the firm: Tripp. Once she thought about it, Tripp's presence wasn't a surprise at all. She knew that he and Ben had been spending time together; they were the same, birds of a feather. Where there was opportunity without effort, there were always men like Tripp and Ben.

In addition to the uninvited attendees, there was also Black Raven, Auntie Layla and her son, and a woman who, based on description, Ehnita assumed was Rea, Wes's new love interest.

"Sister, thank you for coming." Wes walked over to give Ehnita a hug. Posh spotted Black Raven and dashed between the two of them to get to him.

"Hi. Yeah, it's no problem. What's going on?"

Stepping toward her smiling, Ben extended a tube in her direction. "For the bridge. We came up with a proposal. While we could just tear it down, instead we'd like to restore it and use it as a connecting point and attraction. It would mean a huge restorative project, with all the expense being on our client's end, of course, but it would make it safe for all parties involved. It would also mean that we would need to relocate this office, which our client is willing to pay generously to do, but—"

Before he could finish, Ehnita was already shaking her head and throwing her hands up in protest. "No. The bridge stays exactly like it is."

Caught off guard, Ben nervously chuckled and took a step toward Ehnita. "Ana, be reasonable. The bridge is old anyway, and it wouldn't be torn down; it would be replaced with something better."

"Replacing something doesn't make it better. It just makes it new."

From the crowd behind Wes, Ehnita could hear Layla giggle.

"Gentlemen, I am so sorry Ben brought you all the way up here for this. But the bridge stays, the office stays, everything stays."

As she walked toward her client, making her apologies, cutting right into her path was Ben, who stood in front of Ehnita, still smiling but very much annoyed and looking intentionally menacing. "Ana, think clearly about this. It would be more beneficial for all parties involved if everyone got on board with this plan. Once the high-rise goes up—"

His romantic feelings toward Ehnita may have petered away, but his genuine concern and care for her had not, and in that moment, Wes did not appreciate the tone in Ben's voice. Wes stepped forward and stood by Ehnita's side silently as he stared down at Ben, who took a step back.

"There will not be a high-rise on the other side." Pure joy filled Ehnita's cheeks as the words fell from her lips.

Ben huffed and shot Wes a fake smile. "The high-rise is going up whether you like it or not. It would be easier for everyone involved if you just got on board, Sheriff. It's a done deal."

"No, Ben, actually it is not." As she sidestepped to look around Ben, from the corner of her eye, she could see Layla and Black Raven give her an affirming nod.

"What is it with you today, Ana? You come up here dressed like you're ready to clean houses, you bring the dog with you to a business meeting, and now you're telling our client what not to do with their property. Clearly this place is affecting you in a way that neither one of us could see coming. But, Ana, you don't need to feel bad about your decision to sell. You don't have to try to make them happy anymore. It's done. You don't owe them anything."

"It's not done. And you're right, I don't owe them *anything*. I owe them *everything*." Out of patience and done with the pretense, Ehnita snapped. She'd officially had enough. When the project began, all the work was on her, every decision, all the research and mediation and negotiation. Now, when things were *easy* and considered *a done deal*, Ben, who was indifferent in the beginning, was leading the way at the end.

"Ana, listen—"

"It's Ehnita! My name is Eh-Nee-Tah."

"Yes, my Ehnita, you tell them. Tell them to go. We don't want their money or their buildings here." Shaking her fingers at the developers Layla stepped forward and stood by Black Raven's side and scowled at the men who had now become extremely irritated.

"I think you gentlemen should leave my office now." Turning toward the door, Wes nodded in the direction of the exit.

The developer, who did not care to hear any more anyway, jumped at the invitation to leave and headed out the door. Tripp looked at Ben and shook his head. As a partner he should have been furious, but as a rival, he was completely amused. Ben's loss of control over the project as well as his woman meant a win for Tripp. This meeting not only ended a development deal, but it also ended a newly budding and dubious friendship; Ben was no longer an asset when Ehnita became a liability. Tripp had no need for him.

Wanting to offer something of an explanation, Ehnita followed behind the dejected buyer, with Ben on her heels the whole way.

The sky outside had gone from crystal blue to stormy gray. Raindrops began to fall as Ehnita made her way to the town car parked next to her sedan. Before she could speak, Ben's hand was pulling at her arm. "Ana, what the hell is going on with you?"

"I'm not selling, Ben."

"What do you mean you're not selling? You already signed the paperwork days ago. You can't just change your mind."

"I never said I signed anything. I said I reviewed it, and I did. And after my review, I decided not to sell."

The fury coming out of the town car could be felt with the slamming of the door.

"What do you mean, you decided not to sign, Ana?"

"It's Ehnita."

"Fine, fine, Anita. Anita, you told me you signed."

"EH—Ehnita. And no, I never told you that."

"You let me bring everyone up here based on the fact that this was a done deal. You owning the property meant we didn't need anyone else's permission. You can't just change your mind. Do you realize how much money is being invested into this project? You're going to ruin your career, and for what? For this? Some trees, dirt, a dried-up waterfall, and an old bridge? What about me? What about my career? We're supposed to be partners here, for Christ's sake, we're supposed to be getting married, and you go and make this unilateral decision."

Ehnita didn't want to fight. As the rain began to fall harder, she looked at Wes and Black Raven and everyone else who had come out of the office to watch. She studied everyone's faces and she smiled. They didn't say it, but she could feel it: They were proud of her, and they were standing behind her. She was one of them. After taking it all in, Ehnita took a breath and ran to her car to grab the folder she brought with her.

"Auntie." She walked back toward the office, Ben at her heels, still wanting an explanation. Ehnita jogged the rest of the distance between her and Layla, and when she was within reach, she quickly wrapped her arms around her and held her close.

"My Ehnita, your mother would be so proud of you. *I* am so proud of you."

Reluctantly releasing her, Ehnita handed Layla the folder. "It's yours now, Auntie. All of it. Every single acre. You pass it down and keep it in the family."

She knew she had his approval, but she looked at him anyway just to confirm. Smiling as he nodded, Black Raven silently stood watching, his eyes filled with pride. Soaking wet from the rain but happy to be bearing witness, Wes smiled at Ehnita and nodded. She'd done it. She had taken ownership of her inheritance and saved two worlds, as Tatanka had said. She had saved them all. There would be no tearing down, no relocation, not in this generation or the next. Ehnita had chosen her beneficiaries wisely. Layla had three sons and four daughters, all of whom had their own children. The land would be passed down for centuries. No one would be able to build on the land because to Layla and her family, *they* were the land—they were as much a part of it as it was of them. To them the land was sacred, and now Ehnita finally understood why that which was sacred could not be built upon. The tribe would never part with it. The books were right; all of the books were right. That which is considered sovereign can never be bought, because it will never be sold.

"And to you, brother, in there you will also find the title to my condo. I've signed it over to you. It's paid for, as well as my car. Also, I've given Auntie control of all my bank accounts, so don't worry about anything. You and Rea will have everything you need to help as many people as you can. Everything in my condo is yours."

"Everything in that condo does not belong to you, Ana. What about me?" Staring at her in disbelief, Ben slapped his arms at his side in frustration.

Shaking her head and giggling, she turned back around. "Except for Ben's clothes. Be sure to give Benjamin back his clothes. Everything else is at your disposal to help whoever you can."

Honored and grateful, Wes hugged Ehnita as hard as he could without actually hurting her. When he released her, Black Raven came up and stood in front of her and ran his hand over the top of her head and smiled.

"Do you hear it, Moon?"

Light and excitement filled her eyes as she turned her head from Black Raven to the side of the sheriff's office and back again. The sound of rushing water filled her ears, and as she looked up at Black Raven, completely filled with joy, thunder rolled overhead. But to her it didn't sound like thunder; it was a sound that nearly stopped her heart. Roaring across the sky and vibrating in her ears like a thousand lions all at once was Oteitani, and he was calling her name.

Gently holding the side of her face and still smiling, Black Raven looked up to the sky and then back down to Ehnita. "He searches for you, Sky Woman. Go now. Get all that you have been searching for, all that has been left to you."

"I love you, Grandfather." Wrapping her arms around his neck and quickly kissing him on the cheek, she gave him one last look, wanting so badly to take him with her but knowing that she couldn't. As she tilted her head back and took one last look at the sky, rain poured down on her face and she laughed.

She let go of Black Raven's neck, gave him a quick kiss on the cheek again, and then quickly turned around and ran full speed toward the bridge behind the office.

"Ana! Ana! Anita!" Running behind her angry and confused, Ben waved his hands at Ehnita's back. "What are you doing?"

Once she was at the bridge, she didn't cross it. She stepped off to the side and stood near the edge where she could see mist, and then without any hesitation, she spread out her arms and jumped into the sky.

In her dreams, she thought she was falling into darkness, but she knew now she was wrong; she didn't fall, she leapt, jumped right into the sky.

"Ana, don't! Ana!" Standing at the entryway of the bridge, staring down in disbelief, Ben leaned over the side and saw nothing.

"Why are you all just standing there? Somebody do something! Call the police!"

As he walked toward the group of joyous onlookers, he shook his head at them in confusion. Ben turned and looked back at the bridge, extending his hands toward it and then throwing his arms up in frustration.

"I *am* the police." Wes took a step toward Ben, who immediately took a step back. "Ehnita, my sister, she is fine."

"She's not fine. Are you people crazy? You're all crazy, that's what it is. And you drove her crazy. You literally drove her to jump off a bridge."

"You did not see what you thought you saw, Ben. I give you my word, my sister is fine."

Where words were failing Wes, Black Raven stepped forward, placing his hand on his heart, and smiled as he nodded at Ben.

"Moon has returned home."

Before Ben could protest or argue, Black Raven quickly pressed a finger to his lips, commanding silence, and then with the other hand tapping at his ear, insisted that Ben listen. Black Raven looked over the bridge and smiled. "Su-wee!"

Confused and irate and on the verge of a complete meltdown, Ben took a step forward, about to go on an all-out tirade when he heard it. From the bridge, where no one stood, he heard the echo of several voices respond to Black Raven's call.

"*Su—wee!*"

"Heaven and earth have changed places. Moon has inherited the sky. She is home now." Chuckling to himself as he walked away, Black Raven gave a quick pat to his thigh, and from the crowd Posh came running to follow the old man home.

***

"EHNITA!"

With his chest filled with sorrow, and his heart pressed toward the sky, Oteitani shouted as loud as he could, hoping and praying that she would somehow hear him.

"*EHNITA!*"

As Oteitani stood underneath the waterfall at the edge of the cave, suddenly, from out of nowhere, like lightning being captured in a bottle, she was there. Thinking his eyes had deceived him, he stood there staring in sheer amazement at the disruption to the water and nearly burst with joy when he watched Ehnita's head emerge and break the surface of the water as she came up for air. Oteitani didn't waste any time. He dove off the ledge and into the water and swam to her.

Smiling and laughing, Ehnita wrapped her arms around his neck.

"You waited for me."

With his forehead pressed against hers, Oteitani let out a large sigh of relief and stared into Ehnita's eyes.

"Yes. I searched for you, and I waited for you, as I always will."

Still holding him as tightly as she could, Ehnita turned her head and looked toward the shore, and there she could see members of the tribe emerging from the woods, waving and smiling at her. They all came to welcome her home. As they gathered along the water's edge, they hugged each other as they waited to hug her; and in the happiness they found in finding her once again, in unison they all called out to announce her return.

"Su—wee!"

www.ingramcontent.com/pod-product-compliance
Lightning Source LLC
Chambersburg PA
CBHW020657010826
48969CB00013B/2181